The Street King I Fell For:

A Misunderstood Love Affair

By: A.J. Davidson

Dedication

My first book is dedicated to my husband Andre 'Earl', who made sure I had everything I needed to get this book finished. He never fussed when I forgot to cook dinner or clean the house lol because I was so wrapped up in this book. He was just happy that I finally found something to do that I enjoyed. He supported me 110 percent with my writing and I couldn't ask for a better partner. I can't forget about my baby boys Jarrett and Ashton. You two are my entire existence and everything I do is all for you. I can't wait until the kids ask you what your mom does for a living and you say "My mommy is an author". That may seem like nothing to some but to me, that's everything.

Acknowledgments

First and foremost I would like to thank God for giving me this wonderful gift. I always thought doing hair was my calling until I did a Facebook short story challenge with my cousin Kentiqua. After reading my cousin's story I gave it a shot and your girl killed it. I must say I am one of the Blessed ones. Who else can start writing on December 15, 2016, and get signed with Kellz Kimberly Publishing on January 16, 2017? That wasn't nobody but God who made that happen. Oh and with the help of my author Bae, Paris Tranae'. She gave me so much helpful advice. Every time I doubted myself she was there to push me and pull what she knew I had in me out. For that, I will forever be grateful!!

To all of my KKP sisters always remember the sky is the limit, keep dropping dope books. Also, to my wonderful Publisher Kellz Kimberly, thanks for taking a chance on me.

To my family my mama Sharon, step daddy James, my daddy Kevin, stepmother Sharon (yes they have the same name lol) my sisters Alicia "Ree Ree" and Asia, my baby brother Kayin, and a special Auntie Lynne Black, I would like to personally Thank you guys for your support and love. I wish I could name my entire family but just know I appreciate the support from you guys too. Also, my friends and my readers, I want to thank each and every last one of you guys. You guys pushed me to write more short stories and everyone of you shared and helped me gain readers from all over. Thanks for the support and I will continue to put out more books that you will fall in love with. So in my Remy Ma voice "Nothing can stop me, I'm all the way up" and that's exactly where I plan to go from here.

To stay up to date on A.J. Davidson

Facebook: Ashley Johnson Davidson

Instagram: ashleynobankz

Facebook Like page: Author A. J. Davidson

Chapter 1

Cherish "CeCe" Carter

"Aye, sis, get up! I'm about to move around and get ready for work. I don't want to keep waking you up," I said, shaking my sister awake. Karma falling asleep in my bed was normal for us. As usual, we stayed up most of the night talking and laughing trying to figure out our next move and reflecting on all the bullshit we've been through over the years.

"I'm good, I'll just stay here," she mumbled, causing me to shrug my shoulders. That was fine by me.

"Want me to make you a smoothie?" I asked, before heading to the kitchen, only for her ass to start snoring again.

I couldn't help the involuntary mug that crossed my face when my eyes landed on my little sister, Cocoa cooking breakfast in just a pair of thongs. She didn't even have on a bra! She knew I hated that shit and honestly, I think she does the shit on purpose.

"Do you have to walk around like that?" I asked.

"Yep, who gone check me?" she replied, rolling her eyes at me like she's really tough knowing damn well she can't bust a grape.

"Let me rephrase that shit; don't nobody want to see yo ass walk around like that. You need to put on some fucking clothes."

"Hell, we all have a pussy. Mine may be worth more than the one y'all got, but we all have one nonetheless." She shrugged, turning her attention back to the eggs and bacon she was hooking up. I can't lie, he smelled good as fuck but I was on a lil' health kick. Cocoa could eat whatever she wanted because the shit would travel straight to her hips and ass. Sis was stacked but I had to watch out for my shape. I'd mess around and look like I'm six months pregnant. "Besides, I'm confident in my sexuality. Y'all should be too."

"Whatever Cocoa, just put some damn clothes on because I refuse to go back and forth with you," I said as I proceeded to mix my green smoothie as if she wasn't there.

An hour later I was fully dressed in a fitted black midi skirt, a black wrap blouse and a pair of black peep-toe pumps. After quickly combing my hair up into a high bun and slipping on some midi rings, hoops and a nameplate necklace, I was grabbing my keys and bags.

"Karma, you are still coming to fill out more applications, right?"

"Yea, I will be there a little later. I'm just sleepy right now."

"Well here is a few dollars just in case you need to grab something to eat," I replied, throwing two tens on the bed before bumping into Cocoa again on my way out.

"Will I be seeing you at the mall to fill out applications too? We all need to be getting several checks around here." I said, knowing I was wasting my breath. My sister had a sponsor for every day of the week and a nine to five just wasn't in her plans. That's the reason we constantly butted heads.

"Nah I'm good, when you're sitting on a million dollars baby, you never seem to find time to answer to a manager." She started patting at her pussy. "I manage myself and I damn sure don't need you or no one else trying to tell me what I need to be doing. Oh, plus they give checks at jobs. I only accept cash and black cards cause they never get declined or have discrepancies, sis."

"Oh, you're sitting on a million dollars, huh? Make that the last time you use that fucked up shit mama used to say. That shit ain't gone work with me, you gone need a legit job and selling pussy ain't legit. I feel like I let yo ass slide too much and you forget how I give it up. Keep on playing with my emotions and watch how I spazz on yo ass." I mugged her on the way to the door.

"Shit, what's the difference in what I do and what you do? Neither one of us has room to talk if you ask me. It's both illegal," she said, slamming her room door before I could inquire what she meant.

"What is she talking about, CeCe?" Karma asked, standing at my now open room door.

"Nothing, Karma, you know she's always talking stupid, anyway I'm gone. I love you, see you later," I said, heading to my 2009 Honda Accord and doing the dash to work.

Being the oldest sister of three, I had to take on the responsibility of big sister and mom ever since ours ran off and left us a few years ago. Even though I wish I had a life to focus on and time for school and work, it's just not possible. Some days I wondered how I did this on the regular, but I wouldn't dare let them know how I felt. Karma was easy to please and I enjoyed our time together, but that damn Cocoa was an issue. I loved my little sister Cocoa dearly, but she is so damn crazy. She's all about her money, but not in the way I want her to be. I don't understand why she acts the way she does, we used to be close until one day we just weren't. It's like she stopped following me and started following my mom. Her and our mom used to be really close before she left and you can tell she still has some abandonment issues. Ma couldn't move without Cocoa being right on her heels, and she always cried leaving out of the house because she wanted to go with her so badly.

Karma is the middle sister and she wouldn't give two fucks about what I said, she makes things easy. They are both out of high school now so I try to stay on them about finding a job or even enrolling into some type school, instead of lying around looking for someone or some man to take care of them. One thing I try to get them to see is that they are beautiful women and looks won't last forever. As soon as that nigga gets what he wants out of them, his ass will be on to the next piece of cute ass. Education and having your own money is everything. Let these niggas know they are wanted but not needed and that you can hold your own. Karma understands that but then there is Cocoa. She reminds me so much of my mother, it's sickening. My mama tried to instill in us that your pussy paves ways and with Cocoa that stuck. She would rather suck and fuck for a buck than get a legal job. I've tried everything I could to get her to change her mind frame but it was pointless. I had talked until I was blue in the face and it didn't change a damn thing. I made it perfectly clear that I didn't want any of her hoe money and that wouldn't change anytime soon. I worked hard for everything I provided, so her money really wasn't necessary anyway.

***

Walking into work, I greeted my co-workers then made my way to the break room to save my things. I started working at Victoria Secret six months ago and I've already moved up to assistant manager. I'm out here trying to get all the money I can get so I can keep providing for my sisters. I'm trying to keep my head on straight and focus on them. We live in a middle-class neighborhood and I wanted to keep it that way. Before working here, I was basically doing what I could to get by. Any hustle was a good hustle, except selling pussy, if you asked me. I would do whatever to make sure my sisters and I never had to return to the projects.

"Cherish, we have a lil' crowd, can you get out here?" I heard over the earpiece that I had just slipped on. Without responding, I walked out and greeted the first woman I saw.

"Hello, I'm Cherish. If there's anything I can help you with let me know."

"Thanks, I'm just browsing at the moment," she replied.

After making sure everyone else was fine, I began walking around the store, re-folding and re-stocking our new Pink sweatsuit collection. These lil' girls had been buying these up like they are 2 for 1 wet and wavy Malaysian bundles.

"Excuse me, can you help me find this in a 36B?" I heard from behind me.

Standing to my feet and turning around, my eyes landed on a hot ass mess. Lil' mama had blue bundles. Now, I'm not a hater so understand that her shit was laid. That wasn't the problem, those thick ass blue eyebrows and broom sized lashes are what killed me. Nonetheless, I was professional and did my job.

"Sure, right this way. This is from our Bombshell Collection," I said, walking her towards the wall she was looking for. One look at the woman's chest and I knew damn well she couldn't fit no B cup, she was at least a D.

"Here you go. This entire section is B cup, what you asked for. However, I have to ask, are you shopping for yourself?"

"Yeah, I am, is that a problem?" I found myself biting my tongue when she rolled her eyes. "I'm not being nosey, I'm just trying to help. If you don't mind me asking, have you been measured before?"

"No, I always just hold the bra up and see if it looks like it will fit," she answered, demonstrating her process for me.

"I see, that will never be accurate, though. If you would like you can step right in here and I'll measure you so we can make sure you are getting the right size bra."

Without another word, she followed me off to the side so I could grab my tape measure. I watched as she removed her shirt and all I saw was some nice ass breasts. I'm far from gay, but this woman was either blessed or had seen Dr. Curves. I quickly measured her and it was just as I thought.

"Yeah, so no more holding up the bras, you are a 36D."

"Are you sure? I've been in a B cup since high school," she said, cupping her breasts like she didn't believe it herself.

"I'm positive, you can come this way and I'll show you where your size is located on the wall," I said as she slid her shirt over her head.

After helping her, I noticed the store slowed down a little and I found myself watching the clock; good thing I didn't close tonight. I had some things I wanted to buy then I needed Karma to hook up my hair, so I was more than ready to go home. Minutes turned into hours and finally, it was time for me to start my closing out process.

While folding the panties and pajamas at the door, I noticed Karma in the middle of the mall talking to some of her friends and as usual, Cocoa was nowhere to be found.

"Karma, come here!" I called to her, stepping outside of the glass doors.

"Sup, big sis, what time do you get off?" She walked over eating a pretzel from Auntie Ann's.

"I get off in two more hours, but anyway where's Cocoa? Make sure you keep your eyes on her, you know she likes to dip off and I don't want you fighting for her."

"Man, I've got her. You just get back to work. She's good," she assured me before walking away.

"Aight, stay close by, and I ain't playing Karma. NO FIGHTING!" I stressed.

"You do know I'm twenty-two right? That means I'm grown and you don't have to watch my every move," she called over her shoulder as she walked off quick to get out of sight. They loved to complain but knew that I meant well, at least I hope they did. I felt a tap on my shoulder that snapped me out of my thoughts.

"You can leave early if you'd like, we are pretty slow right now." I rolled my eyes before turning to face Patrice, the general manager. Her ass tries to cut back on hours every chance she gets.

"Cool, let me grab my things," I answered, placing a fake smile on my face.

Without another word, I made my way to the time clock, quickly grabbing some things my sisters would love. I noticed the new girl at a register with no customers so I quickly jumped in her check outline.

"Hey, Donna, what time do you get off, ma?" I asked. placing the jumpsuits and fragrances on the counter.

"In fifteen minutes, Patrice told me to leave early. I'm so sick of these cuts and I just started," she replied, rolling her eyes and scanning my items.

"Oh ok, me too; that's why I'm headed out the door now. I just wanted to grab a few things for my sisters. Do you mind typing my card in? It's not swiping that well and I'm waiting on the bank to send me another one," I explained.

"That means you applied too much pressure to that card. It happened to me because I swiped entirely too much." She chuckled, typing in the numbers I called out and handing me my bags. Since I got off work early, I walked around the mall until I found Karma.

"Hey, where's Cocoa? I'm ready to go home," I said as soon as I found her in the food court. The look on her face pissed me off instantly. "Man, what did she do now?" I asked not in the mood for the bullshit I knew was to come.

"Sis, look I'm not about to get in the middle of this. You know how she is."

"What you mean, in the middle of what? Karma, stop playing with me, where is she?" I pressed.

"I think she's with ole dude again."

"Come again? It's so many ole dudes that I'm finding it hard to keep up. Be more specific."

"You know that nigga Lorenz? We just passed him and his lil' bitch who got me fired for beating her ass in the store. As soon as we walked passed Forever 21, he saw us and did a little fucking gesture to her while his girlfriend had her back turned and the next thing I know, she gets a text and said she had to go before I could say anything."

"Where did you say you saw him at again?" I asked ready to find Cocoa.

"Back in Forever 21," she said, following behind me. We made it to the store in no time, but as usual, it was packed.

"We're never going find her in here if she's even here, to begin with," I said, pulling out my phone and calling her again. I already knew she wouldn't answer, so I wasn't shocked to hear her voicemail. Looking around, someone caught my eye. "Karma, isn't that his girl right there?" I pointed at the cute redbone.

"Hell yea, with her fuck boy ass. I outta slide her again for fucking up my money," Karma said, lifting her bundles up into a high ponytail. I grabbed her hand and led her away from the chick cause her ass would seriously fight her off the strength of a flashback.

"I know damn well Cocoa is not in here with her man while this bitch is in the store too," I said, walking around as I made my way to the back of the store. Hearing moans coming out of the dressing room, I said a prayer before bending down to look under the stall. All I saw was a big ass pair of Jordan's, but the moaning gave her away.

"Cocoa, I will smack the fuck outta yo hoe ass if you don't get out here NOW!"

"Waaaaaittt, Ohhhhh….shittttttt I'm cummingggg!" she moaned loudly and all I could do was pray his bitch ain't hear her because I swear I don't feel like fighting tonight; even though Karma's ass is always down to rock any bitch that steps to her sisters.

I banged on the door again until I heard his ass grunt and noticed her Jordan's hit the floor next to his. Can you imagine they had the nerves to rock matching Jordan's like they were a couple? Moments later, the door opened and Cocoa smiled at me. She walked out of the dressing room pulling her dress down, not giving a damn.

"Sup, big sis?" Lorenz said as he adjusted his pants before walking out.

These motherfuckers had on matching fits! Cocoa was rocking a blue t-shirt dress with a white polo button down tied under her breasts and his ass had on blue jeans with the same white polo and blue and white Jordan's.

"Hold up playboy, you know how this goes. You have to pay to play, now run me my money," Cocoa said before he could get too far.

I watched as he licked his lips, then pulled out a bankroll. Without counting, he walked over and slid it in her breasts and tongued her down like his bitch wasn't in this store. With a slap on her ass, he walked back towards his woman who was making her way to where we were standing.

"Cocoa, don't say shit to me while I'm pissed off," I said, cutting her off as she opened her mouth to speak.

"You wanted me to bring a check in, right? So I brought in a check," she said, flashing the money and rolling her eyes like I was playing with her ass

"Don't play, you knew what the fuck I meant! And I don't want your hoe money!" I spat, walking away from her. As we walked out the store, I watched the nigga that was just fucking her, kissing his bitch in her mouth.

"What the fuck? He was just balls deep in you," Karma said to Cocoa, who instantly smiled.

"Tongue deep too," she replied, sticking out her tongue.

The shit wasn't funny if you asked me. Anything could have happened while she was in there getting her ass wet. His girl could have come back there and fucked Cocoa up, or the manager could have come back there with police and had her ass locked up. Cocoa was gorgeous as fuck, but baby girl just didn't think. I try to be a big sister instead of a parent to her, but when she does shit like this the role has to change. Our mom left a while back. At the time, I was twenty-two, Karma was nineteen and Cocoa was eighteen, but before she left, we were pretty much raising ourselves anyway because she hardly came home at night. The bitch didn't have the balls to face us. She simply left a letter that said, *I can't do this anymore, I'm sorry.* The fuck kind of shit is that to tell your kids?

I thought it was a joke and maybe she would be gone for a few days as usual. The joke was on me because days turned into weeks, weeks turned into months and months turned into years. Anytime Cocoa did shit like this she reminded me of my mother. I hate to see my sister go down the wrong path and the way Cocoa is going she will end up just like her. The only relief I got from the day was when I actually made it home with food and a Bud Light. Damn my hair or any of the plans I made, sleep came quickly.

***

I wasn't looking forward to work but it was payday and I had to open. After thirty minutes I was done counting the registers, checking deposits, putting the numbers into the system and had sent everything over to corporate. I thank God for the free time I had to enjoy my Caramel Frappe before the mall opened because I knew that it would get crazy early. I was lost in my thoughts and didn't even notice I wasn't alone in the break room until I felt a tap on my shoulder.

"Shit, you scared me." I jumped with my eyes on my coworker.

"Sorry, girl, but it's after nine and there are customers here. I can't clock on until ten," she replied.

Nodding my head, I stood to my feet and went to greet the customers. Being that I do work for Victoria Secret I was expecting women, but instead, the sight before me made my pussy awaken. It was two of them, but my eyes were only on the one that stepped forward. He looks like he was maybe 6'1, caramel skin, brown eyes, his swag was sexy as hell, he had a tattoo sleeve on both arms and when he stepped forward, his cologne alone had a bitch's knees weak.

"Welcome to Victoria Secret, I'm Cherish, how can I help you today?" I said the rehearsed greeting.

"Peep this ma, I need you to hook me up with all the shit that females like from here, in these sizes," he answered, handing me a paper. Looking down at it, I noticed the sizes varied so they damn sure weren't for one chick.

"Do you want anything in particular? Do you have a budget?"

"Nah ma, you look like you have good taste, just make it sexy. Budget wise, do you," he replied, licking his lips and checking out my ass as I walked around the store.

I loved shopping, so him saying no budget allowed me to cop whatever I felt like. In my mind, I was shopping for me. It's crazy but I've never been spoiled like that so I was living through these women. Less than an hour later, I returned to him and his friend who stood around talking.

"Here, this should look great on all of your women," I replied, handing him the three shopping bags full of underwear, pajamas, robes, fragrances and PINK wear.

"How you figure I have a lot of women?" He smiled, showing a bottom row of golds.

"This," I replied, handing his list back to him.

"Oh naaah, it's nothing like that." His homeboy stood behind him chuckling. He was fine as hell too. I guess it's true when they say birds of a feather flock together.

"What's funny? I like to laugh." I asked them, walking towards the register

"Nothing, don't mind him, Cherish," he said, remembering my name from earlier. I didn't have a name tag on so I was a lil' impressed. I gave a little smile as I turned and looked at him.

"By the way, I'm Eazy and this is my lil' brother Blaise," he said just as another fine ass nigga walked in. "Oh and that's our home boy Chino." He motioned to the man that hit me with a head nod and a smile.

"Good to know, now that will be $724.09, will that be cash or card?" I expected him to question what the fuck I copped for all that but he just slid a card my way without a second thought. His homeboys, however, were wondering why the fuck he spent so much money on some damn— in their words— drawls.

"Aye ma, you can speed this up? I've gotta bounce," he asked, looking at the iced out Rolex on his wrist.

"I do apologize that system wasn't working I had to use another one. Here you are. Y'all have a good day," I answered, sliding the card, receipt and bags his way. Without another word, he was out the store. I helped a few customers here and there but overall it was slow as hell. When I looked up and saw my sisters, I was happy for some entertainment.

"I want to ask why y'all up here so early but then again, I'm just glad someone is here." I laughed.

"I forgot my purse in your car last night. Can I get the keys?" Karma asked.

"Oh ok. Here, bring my keys right back too. Now hurry up, my manager is coming in and I don't want her to see you guys hanging out in the store." No sooner had they walked out, Patrice walked in. The look on her face wasn't pleasant, but then again, it never was.

"Hey, Cherish, I'm glad we are here alone, I need to talk to you," she started as soon as she was in my face.

"Umm, ok. Is everything good, Patrice?" I questioned.

"Actually, I can't say that it is. I noticed some consistent discrepancies in your paperwork, particularly on the money side. It's short on the nights you close and a few days later when you open all of a sudden things balance out. I like your work ethic but it's out of my hands. Effective immediately, we are putting you on a temporary suspension until we figure out what going on," she said, causing me to awkwardly laugh.

"Are y'all accusing me of stealing? I know I do the same thing every time I open and close and I've been doing this for a while now, so I'm not sure where the error is coming in at," I defended myself.

"We will get it all sorted out but here is your last check and I will call you once we get it together. The truth always comes out," she assured me.

"Ok, well, I'll be waiting for that call and an apology," I said, grabbing my things from the back and walking out.

Leaving the store, I racked my brain of ways I can come up on some money real quick. I know Cocoa can hold her own, but I have to make sure Karma and I are straight and make sure these damn bills are paid. I could do like I did when my mother left; max out every card I had so I could resale the shit for cash. Maybe I can try to get a few payday loans or something too. One thing I was not going to do is ask Cocoa for any damn thing. I was good on savings for now, but there was no telling how long that would last.

"Are you on lunch?" Karma asked as I met them at the car.

"Nah, get in. I've gotta talk to y'all," I said, starting the car. "Cocoa, Karma, look shit is about to change around here. I need help for a lil' while so that we don't fall behind on bills and have to dig into our savings."

"What's wrong, sis?" Karma asked, she hated seeing me frustrated.

"I got suspended today and until they finish this dumb ass investigation on me, I'm out of a job. Apparently, they are thinking I'm stealing money or some shit." I shrugged it off.

"Well…"

"Well, what Karma? Say what's on your mind, fuck!" I spat at her. The situation already pissed me off and the last thing I need is her ass looking sideways at my ass after I took care of her.

"Well, hell, were you, Ce?" she questioned like I owed her some type of explanation.

"Maaaann… You know what? Yep, I sure did! How do you think shit gets done around here, off of sorry ass Victoria Secret? You think we live in that three bedroom, two bathroom apartment on the South off of $12 an hour? You think y'all stay fresh, fed and laid off of $12 an hour? Nope, I didn't think so," I finished, speeding home. The car ride was silent and gave me chance to calm down.

"Sis, it's not like I wasn't working and helping you before, and I would've still had a job if I wasn't fighting for Cocoa," Karma explained after we walked in the house.

"Cocoa and Karma, look, I'm sorry for blowing up on you but I need y'all to grow up. You're twenty-one and twenty-two years old. Y'all know that mama ain't coming back and we're out in this bitch alone. We are all we got and all I'm asking for is more help, legit help," I stressed, turning towards Cocoa.

"We get it, sis, we get it. Sorry!" said Karma.

"Speak for yourself. If legit is what you're looking for, don't look here. I'm allergic to that word," Cocoa said sarcastically, while rolling up a blunt.

"Oh, so you think this shit is a game, huh? Since you've got so much money, tell me Cocoa, why are you still living with me?" I spat.

"Real talk, y'all need me more than I need y'all. Neither one of y'all do shit for me anyway. You think I don't notice how close you two are? Trust me, there have been plenty of times I've thought about leaving, but I can't because deep down, like real deep down, I love y'all. But you and Karma sit around here and talk about me all day like I ain't shit and like I ain't got feelings. Y'all frown on me and call me weak when I'm the strongest bitch standing. I don't remember not one time mama got y'all out the bed to go fuck someone so she can get an eight ball or a few pounds of Kush. Cherish, answer me, how many dicks you had to suck before the age of twelve? Karma, how many unknown men have been inside of you by the time you were fifteen? Don't rush those answers, I'll fucking wait. I was taught to fuck and get money and I grew accustomed to that shit. Every time I offered you money to help you with bills, rent or your car getting fixed, you always turned me down and I went right in my room and put that shit up thinking one day she will need me. Well, surprise, today is the day. Ce, I've got over twenty stacks in my room now just waiting for you to say "Sis, I need help" and that's all the shit that you turned down and I never touched that shit. But that makes me the bad guy, huh? You know what? Fuck it and fuck y'all. No matter what I tell you, you both will only judge me." Cocoa finished, slowly walking into her room and slamming the door. When it rains it pours. If I knew where my mama was, I would kill the hoe myself.

Chapter 2

Elijah "Eazy" Johnson

"Yooooo."

"B, I'm coming through," I told my brother.

"It's good, I'm at the crib. I've got a few bitches over cooking me a feast," he replied to the females whipping work. I warned his ass about that shit.

"Aye, what did I tell you about letting bitches know where you live? They ain't gotta cook for your ass over there. That's the quickest way to get yo ass set up or robbed and their asses killed. Tell them hoes they gotta go now nigga and clear that shit out!" I heard beeping and realized his childish ass clicked me.

My little brother Blaise is twenty-three and his ass still doesn't think before he does dumb shit like this. Niggas looking for a come up and he's helping them easily. These niggas around here already screaming the streets ain't eating, like we're keeping them from making money. Hell, we got the same twenty-four hours in a day, I ain't about to give a nigga or a bitch shit. You want that work? I got that work and right now my brother Chino and my cousin Rocko are the only niggas I trust. Rocko was born and raised in New York. Our moms are sisters and they both had a baby by brothers. Rocko and I look more like brothers than Blaise and I. Rocko is running shit out there and making major moves. You can't breathe in that city without word coming back to him that you took a breath without asking him. He was that nigga for real. He taught me how to run this shit here, but Memphis is so small compared to where he is. Instead of a nigga respecting you, they would rather murder you and take yo shit. The main reason why I stay on Blaise's ass about having hoes in his house is you can't trust their asses either. Pulling up to Blaise's crib, I see him and Chino through the window still breaking down shit like I didn't tell him clear that shit out.

"This nigga!" I said, rubbing my hand over my face. "Why the fuck would he have the blinds and shit all open so motherfuckers could see him. I swear he ain't gone ever learn. I've got something for his ass, though," I said aloud to myself.

Not once did he even look up and see my truck pulling in. I quickly reached under my seat and pulled out my .9 and walked around the back. Slowly twisting the doorknob, I made my way in without a sound. These niggas didn't even have the door locked. They had the game on his 60-inch TV up so fucking loud that even if I did make a noise they wouldn't hear shit.

"Get yo bitch ass up and give me yo work and yo fucking money!" I said while grabbing Blaise around his neck and putting my gun to his head. Chino looked and saw it was me then chuckled.

"Aye, man, don't do no shit like that!" Blaise said as I let him go. I already knew he was pissed when he jumped up ready to fight. Dropping my gun and lifting my pants, I was gonna rock his ass until Chino stood between us.

"That shit was foul!" Blaise screamed.

"Nah, Joe, I told you one too many times about being aware of your surroundings. You could have easily had your shit blown the fuck off. WHY THE FUCK IS THE DOOR UNLOCK AND THE WINDOWS OPEN?"

"You ain't my daddy, I know how to handle my shit if a nigga comes in my crib," he childishly answered.

"But, you couldn't handle me, though. We've got a spot by the lake to do this shit at, why the fuck didn't you go there?"

"Cause I didn't feel like driving way out there." He shrugged.

"That's some bitch shit for real, Blaise. Come on and clean this shit up! Rocko is flying in today to check on some shit and look how you moving. I'm about to pick his ass up and you know if he sees this shit, you're gone really have to square up with him. You know that nigga is just like me, he doesn't play that shit."

"That's on his body, that nigga doesn't pump fear in my heart," he said but started cleaning the shit up.

Moments later, we were loading up in my truck. Riding down to the airport, for some reason, shorty was on my mind. I had been thinking about her ass for a few days now. She was fine as hell with her juicy ass lips, looking like she could deep throat all of this dick. Lil' mama had a banging ass body and her greenish-brown eyes had my ass in a trance for real.

"Say, bruh what cho ass over there smiling out the window and playing these sad ass love songs for? You're supposed to be so damn hard, but you riding around here listening to some old ass

Tyrese "Sweet Lady", turn this shit off and put that new Jeezy on," Blaise said, making me side eye his hating ass.

"Fuck you, my guy, this is my truck." I laughed while grabbing my phone to change the song. "Blaise, you remember shorty from Victoria Secret, Cherish?"

"Yea, the bitch was bad. Too slim for my taste, though," he answered, nodding.

"Watch your mouth. But peep it, shorty's been on my mental heavy, I've gotta get at her lil' ass and see what she's about."

"Mannnn, ion trust no black bitch with green eyes. I'm telling you now, you can't trust them hoes."

"What the fuck do her eyes have to do with it?" Chino asked, while laughing at his dumb ass and actually waiting on a fucking answer, I didn't even want to hear the shit because I knew he was coming with something crazy.

"E, check it. The only people who are supposed to have green eyes are white people. So if I run into a black bitch with them, nigga I'm going back the other way. If she's stealing folk's eye color, she can steal anything," he finished like that shit made sense.

"Maaan, what book did you read that shit in?" Chino was in the back laughing at this dumb ass nigga too. "I should smack the fuck outta you for saying that shit and thinking it's facts. You must have found the shit on Yahoo, cause I know damn well Google ain't tell you that shit."

Shaking my head, I turned my music up on his ass. I'ma let him sit there and think about that. Blaise was a hot head, he was so quick to pop off at the mouth like he knew everything. He dropped out of school his senior year all because he didn't want to do the exit project, homeboy had a 4.0 GPA and never studied for one test. He was just a naturally smart muthafucka but he was so smart that he was dumb. This nigga will know just by looking at cash if you shorted his ass or not. People knew not to play with him when it came to the money. Pulling up to the pick-up section of the airport, I couldn't help but get a chuckle or two out at the expense of my nigga.

"Look at this nigga, he's dressed like he still in New York," I said to Blaise and Chino before I rolled down my window and yelled out to Rocko. "Nigga it's warm as shit if you don't take that big ass jacket and those Timbs off!"

'That ain't a jacket, E. That's a coat," Chino said, laughing at this nigga dressed like he in below zero weather.

"You're in Memphis now, it's hot as hell here. I know yo nuts are sweating," he said as we cracked up.

"Maaaan, fuck you! And don't worry about my nuts. I've got a bitch for that!" Rocko yelled out while we laughed at his ass. He opened the front door where Blaise was sitting and told his ass to get in the back.

"Nigga, you better close this door because I ain't moving," Blaise said while trying to pull the door from Rocko's hand. Rocko is 6'0 of solid muscle and Blaise's ass is over here looking like a light skin Soulja Boy by the body.

"Blaise, if you don't stop. You're about to break your fucking arm off, bruh," I said, laughing at his ass as he got out and went to the back.

"Sup cuz, I appreciate the pickup, but take me to my crib so I can get in my whip. I ain't trying to get caught in yo shit," Rocko said, causing me to side eye his ass.

"Nah, you're riding with me, my nigga. We got the same damn truck, fuck you mean."

"My shit is black, though," Rocko said as if he was really making a valid point.

My truck is white and I knew he hated riding in white cars which is why I pulled that shit out instead of my black Hell Cat – Dodge Charger. He's got this weird idea that the police notice you faster in white cars. You could tell he and Blaise were kin because they both said some dumb shit at times.

"We're about to grab something to eat then I'll drop you off," I said, going in the opposite direction from his spot.

"Nah, that won't work. I've got shit to do and eating ain't on my agenda right now. You know I'm all about my money first." His big ass complained until I said the magic words.

"My treat."

"Myyyy nigga, why didn't you just say that to begin with?" he said, laughing knowing damn well his fat ass was hungry

"That's what I thought, we can get to the money in a minute. Plus I need to holla at you about some shit, because you know when you get out this truck yo ass gone be ghost until it's time for you to leave," I said as he began nodding.

"You know where to find me, though. One call and I'm in route."

"That's not the point, whoever shorty is you be fucking with has your head gone when you come here. It's a good look for you, though."

"Where we going to eat at cause y'all nigga's ain't talking about shit," Blaise said while leaning up from the back."

"Just sit back and ride. Yo ass ain't paying for it so if I pull up to Wendy's yo ass better be satisfied, my nigga," I replied after turning down my radio so he could hear me clear and understand this is my shit.

"Shit, I wanna know too," Chino replied.

"Aye, you still got the Uber app on your phone, bruh?"

"Yea, why what's up?" I pulled over and made both of their asses get out the truck and drove the fuck off. This wasn't anything new, I stayed kicking their asses out. All the fuck they do is complain.

I rode around for about ten minutes running it with Rocko before I came back. Their asses were still standing there big mad looking like their mama forgot to pick them up from school.

"Get y'all punk asses in the truck. All these hoes y'all fuck with and trick off on and you couldn't call one," I said to Chino.

"I could've, but why do that when I knew you would come back for me?" His ass shrugged as he hopped back in the truck.

"Now, I'm ready to tell y'all where we going. We going to Newks," I said, holding in my laughter cause I knew these niggas hated that spot but it was my shit.

'Newks!" they all said like they were the Doublemint triplets.

"Nigga, fuck that, you can drop me off!" Rocko yelled out as I died laughing. "I need me a damn juicy ass steak and you're talking about some fucking Newks. What the fuck is my big ass gone do with that dry ass salad? That's some bitch food!" he snapped pissed off. Turning my music up, I did the dash all the way to Texas Roadhouse. Fuck them, Newks was the shit.

***

"So yeah, like I was saying you got mad respect in New York and I respect that. These niggas here are so money hungry and don't give a damn how they get it. I already had to lace some bitch and her nigga shit cause they approached me on some police shit while I was getting gas, I tried to fuck their whole world up." I laughed listening to Blaise's ass recall that story.

"Why don't you get out this small ass town anyway? Too many niggas know you here, so you already know the police are watching you and ole hot head ass, Blaise. Come to New York, I've got you. I guarantee you a nigga's gone have too much food to eat when you touch down."

"Not a bad idea, my guy, I will think about that shit," I replied, nodding my head. There wasn't shit keeping me here so it wasn't a bad idea at all.

"You need anything else?" I was interrupted by the waitress as she rubbed her flat ass on my arm while taking some plates off the table.

"Damn, she ain't even ask us if we wanted anything. We're here too, Miss Lady bitch," Blaise rude ass said aloud.

"She had a better chance with y'all niggas anyway," I replied, looking down at her ass. "She ain't my type at all, B." I had my eye on someone so that lil' ass wasn't doing shit for me at all.

"Y'all are not about to talk about me like I'm not standing here!" she snapped with her voice laced with attitude.

"That's cause you ain't here. You're taking this card and paying for our shit," I said sliding the card and ticket back.

"Y'all niggas call us rude in New York but y'all are hell down here," Rocko said, laughing. "Anyway, I'm ready to grab my wheels. You know I've gotta go check my spot out and then I'm gone pop up on my girl."

"Oh, shit speaking of which, I'm supposed to meet up with this chick I met at the mall the other day, so I plan to be knee deep in some pussy by 9:05," Chino said while looking at his black MK watch.

"I guess it's just me and Blaise then. I'm about to take this nigga to our spot on the lake myself so he can get there with no fucking problem and don't have an excuse to not take his ass there to work."

"What you mean, he be working at the house?" Rocko asked as he looked over at Blaise who simply nodded. "What's rule number one, B?"

"What I'm not about to do is get pop quizzed on my shit. I'm a grown ass man, and I can handle my shit without the interference. Save me the conference y'all got brewing, the shit won't happen again," Blaise said before pulling out his phone.

"Fuck what you're talking about! What we're not going do is keep having these conversations! Nigga, y'all are at the top of the food chain here. Unless yo ass has got a death wish, you need to dead that shit and quickly!" Rocko spat.

Typically, I would never let a nigga talk to Blaise like that, but Rocko wasn't just any nigga. His heart was in the right place with this shit, we were all we got and we needed to protect that. Rocko was like our big brother; he was twenty-eight, three years older than me and we respected him. At least Chino and I did. He put us on all this shit and the last thing he needs is Blaise bringing more attention our way.

"Aye, this bitch ain't too bad looking," Chino said as the waitress made her way back with a huge smile on her face.

"Just like I'm not your type, you aren't mine. I'm sorry but your card declined," she said loudly, causing people to look our way.

"Lower your fucking voice, and I'm positive you got the wrong nigga. Try that shit again."

"I tried it three times, I even wiped it on my pants leg and it still didn't go through," she repeated what Kevin Hart said from one of his movies like the shit was a joke or something, I almost spazzed out on her ass for thinking shit was funny. "Money problems happen you know," she said before giggling. Standing to my feet, I pulled a bankroll from my pocket before peeling off two hundred dollar bills and throwing them in her face.

"And run me my fucking change, cause the only tip I have for your dumb ass is that when your head goes left, them dry ass tracks should follow. Those bitches have been stuck on froze since I walked in," I said as she stormed off. After getting my change and giving the tip to the waitress at the next table, we dipped. Driving to Rocko's place, I racked my brain trying to remember when was the last time I used that card.

"You got money problems, cuz?" he asked after a while.

"No, I'm good. I just used my card the other day and shorty was having trouble swiping it then, too."

"Are you sure she was having trouble? That bitch probably swiped yo shit for real."

Shorty popped in my head again; she was fucking with my shit a minute talking about one machine wasn't working, so she had to run it on another one.

"I told yo ass about fucking with them green eyes," Blaise said while blowing smoke out his nose.

"This some shit for real. I'm about to go to the mall, right now, this bitch about to catch these hands," I said, feeling played.

"Bruh, you can't hit a bitch." Chino laughed.

"You're right, but I can choke a hoe and make her die a lil' bit."

"Man, bruh. I've gotta see the bitch who finessed you out of all yo bread," Rocko said while laughing like the shit was funny.

Chapter 3

Chloe "Cocoa" Carter

"Look, here's the money I have to help out with the bills. I don't want to hear about how I got it, just take it," I said, handing a roll of money to Cherish.

"No, I don't want your money," she replied, instantly pissing me off.

"I'm only going to offer it to you one more time because I can easily go get my own shit right now. I told you already I don't need to be here! This money ain't shit, there is more where this comes from. I could have gotten my own spot ages ago!" I spat.

"And what happens when those niggas get tired of yo ass?"

"They probably are tired of me, but they ain't leaving, though. They ain't here for me to begin with, it's the power of the pussy. So if I magically go broke and can't afford my spot, I bet you I've got a nigga I'm fucking with who has a black card who can. And baby, we know they never decline! I only stay with you because you always pull that shit about sticking with family, even though you haven't stuck by me not once. Take the money or I take my ass on. Either way, I won't be questioned about how I handle my business anymore."

"What the fuck ever, put the money on the table and I'll get to it later," she said it like she had another option. Her savings wasn't as deep as she wanted us to believe, so she needed me.

Doing as she requested, I threw the money on the table then made my way to the bathroom. Getting in the tub to wash my ass before my session, I pulled out my favorite water toy to play with; I was a certified nympho. Next to money, sex was the most important thing in my world. All I think about is sex, hell even when I'm having sex I'm thinking about the next time I will have sex again. The ringing of my phone ruined my mood and my nut when I noticed I was running late. After quickly washing off and dressing, I grabbed my purse and was on my way out before my name was called.

"I didn't know you were heading out, but I'm thinking we need to sit down and discuss the problems we have."

"I don't have a problem sis. What I do have, however, is an appointment that I'm running late for," I said, looking at my Rolex— a gift from some married man.

"Who is it this time?" CeCe asked.

"Wouldn't you like to know? Since you're in my business, whip out that laptop and fill out applications. I can't be the only one bringing in money, now can I?" I replied while slamming the door behind me.

I was so tired of her ass judging me. She can act like she forgot how I got this way, but I never will! Since I had an appointment, I hit up one of my regulars and he delivered. Sitting in the driveway was this nice ass Challenger he dropped off for me to use. It was his personal car and he let me use it while he went out of town. After all I've done for his ass, this is the least his ass could do. Grabbing the keys from the glove compartment, I started her up and smiled at the sound. Damn this car was sexy, we needed to fuck in this bitch. After rushing through traffic, I finally pull up at Dr. King's office. This was my fifth visit to a therapist, but my first time seeing him. I rushed inside with minutes to spare and was pleasantly surprised by him. I thought he would be another old ass man, but his ass had me wanting to get down with the swirl.

"Hello, Miss Carter. It's nice to meet you," he said, standing to his feet and shaking my hand.

"Nice to meet you as well, Dr. King," I purred.

"Would you rather the chair or the couch?" he asked, motioning to the comfortable looking couch."

"Oh we can do it anywhere, I'm not picky." I smiled as he turned red from my double meaning, but I made my way to the couch where I decided to lay down.

"Ok, I'm going to begin the recording now." He paused to set up then crossed his legs and began questioning me. "I see you've had over four therapists already and I am now your fifth," he said while grabbing a pen to take notes. "What happened with those?"

"Well, I see you guys to discuss my addiction that I can't seem to shake. Every time I get a male therapist and he hears my story, eventually, something happens and I have to find another one after that. Well, I shouldn't just say males cause I really don't have a preference. Honestly, anybody can get it." I shrugged.

"What do you mean, can get what?" He was sitting here looking all puzzled in the face like he didn't already read the reason why my ass is up in here.

"Maybe we should save this question for later," I suggested.

"You know what, just begin telling me what's going on from the beginning, so I can help as much as possible. Now, lay back on the couch and close your eyes and just let everything flow out. Begin where you would like," he said.

"You know I used to be scared of sex. Terrified. I thought those big ole dicks would rip me in two. But I also remember when I fell in love with sex; it was the first time I took two guys at once.

I was sold to some big ass Mandingo having ass men by my own mother. She was on drugs, heavy. So when they offered her a week's worth of drugs to sample me, she was all for it. Now, this wasn't the first time I popped my pussy for her to have a hit and it wouldn't be the last. What made this time different is I actually wanted to fuck them, I needed to. It had been a month since she sold me and I was having these unexplained urges. I know now that I was just horny, but at fifteen, I couldn't understand why my pussy was dripping wet and pulsating. So when she walked in with these two thugged out ass men, I damn near drooled at the mouth. I was sitting there looking like a grown ass woman because before they came, she made sure she pulled me to the side and got me right. My hair was pulled up in a bun and I sat there in lingerie that I'm sure she had stolen because it was so expensive looking."

"Did these men know your age?" Dr. King interrupted me.

"Maybe they did and then maybe they didn't. I'm not sure it would matter anyway, in the hood it rarely does. As long as I was deemed fuckable then that's just what it was. Thanks to the previous men that fucked me, I was already super thick so I easily passed for eighteen.

Anyway, after getting me together for the men, my mama sat me down and told me some bullshit about how she needed me to do her this favor so she could be happy. I wanted nothing more than for her to be happy, so I agreed. Hell, if I would have said no, she would have made me do it anyway. In fact, I wanted her high. She was so mellow when she was high and when she wasn't, she would get angry and hit one of my sisters even if they just asked her a question. My mom gave me a shot of liquor and a pill that she introduced to me as X, then told me to relax and that it was just like the rest of the men, but this time it's two of them.

The room they rented had a bedroom and living area. She told me she would be right outside the door and then she left me to calm down after instructing me to rub KY Jelly on myself. She sat on the couch smiling like she had just won the fucking lottery or something when she heard the guys knocking at the door. After throwing her a bag of shit, they spoke for a minute then she sent them to the bedroom where I was laying on the bed with my pussy dripping and it wasn't from the KY. While I was rubbing it in, I actually started liking the feeling. That was the first time I ever touched myself in that way besides if I'm washing my ass, you know?

So, they walk in and I'm ready like I had never been more ready for anything in my life. My mom had coached me on how to please a man and all that good stuff. I know that me looking scared would be a turn off so I sat with my legs crossed showcasing my thick ass thighs. The heels I wore made my legs go on for days.

With no greeting or anything, one came over to the bed I laid on and started taking his pants off, he couldn't even get his dick all the way out before I made my way to him. I had never been aggressive before, but in that moment I took control. I slapped his hand out the way and simply bent at the waist before I started slurping on it, getting it ready. His dick must have been a good ten inches and I tried to swallow it whole. I now know that pill had me on ten. I had his dick so far down my throat it looked like my chin had balls, Dr. King," I said as I stopped to laugh. Reliving this memory always made my pussy yearn for the experience again.

"Continue with your story," Dr. King urged.

"Where was I? Oh yeah… *I'm bent at the waist taking him all in and I feel the other guy behind me. I was ready for him to take me but he surprises the shit out of me and does something no man had done before. He licked me from my pussy to my asshole. That drove me crazy but he didn't stop there, he ripped my panties off and began fucking my pussy with his thick ass tongue. I remember screaming for dear life and my mama screamed back "that's right baby, take that dick!"*

Now the guy behind me with the hurricane tongue— let's call him dude— Dude was stealing the show and the one I was sucking— let's call him Sir— didn't like that shit. With no warning, Dude lifted me up and placed me right on his rock hard dick. I know my pussy was tight so his ass had to stretch me out and then just held me there for a second, but the pill and my pussy had a mind of their own as I started riding his ass like a carousel on its highest speed. I had him moaning like a bitch and could hear my mama screaming that I was her girl and to take that dick over and over again. Sir couldn't take me but Dude was back there stroking his dick just waiting for his turn. As I rode Sir, I stared in Dude's eyes. I couldn't wait to taste his dick. It turns out Sir had all that dick for nothing, he couldn't hang. Within minutes, he was lifting me up and coming on himself. He laid back to catch his breath, but I had other plans.

I made my way to Dude and begin swallowing his dick whole. His was around the same length yet fatter with a dangerous curve. The way he stroked that monster let me know he knew what he was doing with it too. He attempted to guide my head with his hands like I was an amateur, so I showed him what I could do. Within minutes, I was swallowing his kids, but he was far from done with me. Dude lifted me up and forced his dick so far in my pussy that I was waiting for it to come out of my mouth. My body was momentarily paralyzed but that didn't stop him from hitting me with death strokes. My legs were wrapped around his waist and his hands were wrapped around my neck. Damn, I think it was at that moment I fell in love with dick. Dropping me down, I bent over and I took Sir in my mouth while Dude began fucking me from the back. I started throwing it back even harder, showing him I could take it all. He took his dick out and started cumin' on my back as the other one made sure I swallowed every drop. They changed positions and we fucked for hours. I'm sure I had paid off my mom's debt but I didn't want it to end. The only reason we stopped was because their asses were drained," I finished while laughing.

"Was that the last time you saw them?" the therapist asked as I continued to lay across this cute soft ass couch. He just didn't know my pussy was throbbing just from telling that story all over again.

"Hell no. In fact, I'm in Dude's car today," I honestly answered. Dude and I became kind of a thing after that session. He would never wife me but if the money was right, then so was the pussy.

"And what is you and your mother's relationship now?" he asked.

"I haven't seen her in years, to be honest but I'm fine with that. I don't hate her or any of that shit."

"I see. So—," he began before I cut him off.

"I'm ready to answer your question from earlier now. Do you know why you're the fifth doctor this year?" I asked, sitting up and allowing him to see my bare pussy. All of this sex talk had my juices leaking on his couch.

"Umm…" He began clearing his throat. "Ok, tell me."

"I would rather show you," I said, slipping from the couch and making my way in front of him.

I noticed a while ago how he was really feeling my story but covering his hard dick up by crossing his leg over. He had this big ass bulge in his slacks. He must be free balling cause I could see the head of his dick on the side of his thigh. I began undressing in front of him.

"No, no, you must stop. We can't do this. I seriously can lose my job behind this, Chloe. This is against my firm's guidelines. It's unethical, I just can't do it." The more he told me to stop, the more clothes I took off. While trying to move around the room whispering anything he could to get me to stop, I cornered him by his desk.

"Cut the shit, you can't get fired if no one knows. No one else is here, I have a late appointment. We both know you want to fuck me, so just let me make you feel good. I promise you, this pussy is life changing," I finished before putting my hands down his pants and rubbing on his dick. I smiled when I noticed he stopped moving and was biting his lip. He eyes began to roll to the back of his head like it was feeling good. Seeing the excitement in his eyes, he gave in and started pulling my 38DD breasts out and began sucking on them.

Snatching his shirt open, I pulled myself closer to him pressing my tits up against his chest while sucking on his neck. He slipped his finger into my wet pussy, pulled it out, licked it and put it back in. Lifting me up on his desk and wrapping my legs around him, I started pushing the pictures of his wife and kids onto the floor. Thrusting himself in and out of me, he was long stroking this pussy and every time he came back in my body, it would quiver. Whoever the fuck started that rumor about white men was a goddamn lie. I came over and over and for the first time, I started to squirt. Dropping down to his knees, he put my pussy in his mouth like it was the last supper. I had no idea white men could fuck like this. If I did, I would have been fucking the shit out of them a long time ago. After slurping on my pussy like he hadn't drunk anything in days, he slid his dick right back in and fucked me silly. It wasn't long before he was emptying his seeds in me. If I wouldn't have known any better, I would say he purposely tried to fertilize a fucking egg. As soon as he started nutting, he forced himself in me deeper then continued pumping.

Once we finished, he went into his bathroom and got himself together; me being the person I am, I just pulled a pack of baby wipes out my purse, I'll shower when I get home.

"That was a great session Chloe, a perfect session," he said while I was walking to the door.

"I guess I'm on to therapist number six now, huh?" I said while pushing my breasts up and adjusting them into my bra.

'No, I want you to stick around a while, so same time next week. Free of charge of course," he stumbled over his words.

"Sure, but next time bring cash, that was on the house. Oh, also delete that recording," I replied, smiling as I left out the building.

See why I couldn't get any help with my problem. I tried once before to stop fucking so much, but I really enjoy it. If I'm having a bad day all it takes is a good fuck and a couple of stacks thrown at me and then I forget about whatever pissed me off. That's why I couldn't get down with my sisters, they blamed me for how I was and never cared to know the truth. They were just so busy judging me and I didn't have the time for it. Suddenly, I heard a horn from a car blowing snapping me out of my thoughts, I didn't realize I was sitting at a stop sign by my house. Looking up, I was shocked at the sight before me. We never let niggas come to our crib, that rule was created for me.

Who are these niggas walking up to our apartment? I asked myself while walking up the stairs towards them. It was two men, one it looked like I noticed from around the way, I don't know who the other guy was but they looked so much alike that they kind of looked like twins.

"Umm, are y'all lost or something?" I asked from behind them.

"Yea, I'm looking for a thick, black bitch with green eyes who steals people credit cards. You kinda look like her, do you wear contacts?" the guy that looked familiar asked, while walking up close to me like he was trying to look at my eyes.

"Could you back the fuck up, and who the fuck still wear color contacts?" I spat, stepping back from him.

"I went to her job at Victoria Secret and they said her thieving ass lives up here," he stated.

"Well, I guess they lied because only I live here. And trust, stealing ain't my cup of tea."

"Yea, ok if I find out she's here then we're all gone have a problem, if you see a bitch that fit her description tell her ass Eazy is looking for her," he said while walking back down the stairs to his truck. Once he said his name, I realized where I knew him from. He is the biggest dope boy in Memphis and wasn't to be fucked with.

"Yo boy is gone, so why are you still standing here staring at me?" I snapped at this big ass nigga in front of me.

"Ma, you're real reckless at the mouth. You must not know who I am, my name is Rocko," he said like I gave a fuck.

"Well, Rock yo ass on down the stairs. Like I said, I live alone so the bitch y'all looking for ain't here," I said quickly going into the house and closing the door behind me. I walked into Cherish's room where she and Karma were knocked out.

"CeCe, get up. I need to talk to you now," I stated, shaking her and pushing Karma's ass out the way. "Ce, get up now, for real."

"Why the fuck you making all that noise?" she snapped. Her ass hated people waking her up.

"What's up is yo dumb ass stole from the wrong motherfucker. Eazy and some arrogant ass nigga just left from over here looking for a black bitch with green eyes. Do you know anyone that fits that description?" I sarcastically asked.

"I don't know what you talking about." She tried lying like I was green to her scam. I peeped her jacking credit cards ages ago.

"Keep playing dumb, let's see if he believes that when he comes back. Cause I'm positive he didn't believe my ass. They're gone fuck you up," I said over my shoulder heading to my room. She could play if she wants, but I heard about his reputation and Eazy wasn't anything to play with.

Chapter 4

Romello "Rocko" Johnson

"Say cuz, what's going on, are you good?"

"Yea man, I'm good. I just got a lot on my mind. I'm thinking about letting this shit go. I've been in this game for a long time. If I retired right now at twenty-eight, I'll be straight for the rest of my life. I even have money put up for my kids, kids.

"You got kids I don't know about?" Eazy asked with a confused look on his face.

"Nigga, no! I'm just saying, I've always been taught to think long term, my dad did it for me and I'm doing it for mine. You got this lil' money shit going on here with this bitch. I would've been found her ass, took my bread and killed her. How much she get anyway?"

"I had just started putting money in that account, so it was only like $5,000. The rest is stashed in my crib under the house," Eazy replied.

"I know damn well you don't have me out here hunting a bitch for five stacks, E. Nigga, I could have given you that back." I laughed but I was slick pissed off at him.

"It's not even about the money; it's the principle, Rocko. Don't steal from me!" Eazy spat, "I feel you though. I guess you got that part from my pops, he hated that shit too!"

"Right, but let's get back to shorty. What did she say after I left, you stayed up there a minute?"

"Shit, she said she live alone, but I don't believe that shit at all. Ole girl in the mall was too sure she stayed there, so I know this bitch is lying."

"Nah, I believe her," Chino said from the back seat.

"What? You believe her? Yo gullible ass probably believe pigs can fly too, huh?"

"Nope, but I can tell when I'm being lied to and she ain't lying."

"You know you're one of the smartest niggas in the world right, can't nobody get shit passed you."

"Yea I know. I hear that a lot."

"I thought you said you could tell when you're being lied to?" We laughed at Chino's foolish ass.

This nigga is always in people shit, I don't even see how cuz still fuck with his ass. I closed my eyes and let my seat back some more to tune their asses out. Shorty was cute as hell, she kind of look like Ashley Banks. She was thick like peanut butter, nice juicy ass titties and long black curly hair with a feisty ass attitude, but if she is kin to the black bitch with green eyes, then I may want to stay away from her ass. There ain't no telling what she's capable of. Anyway, my girl Dorian and I have been kicking it for a minute now and I need to be making my way to her ass right now. I've got her staying in my condo and she was having some family issues.

"Say E!" I spat, breaking the silence in the car, "I want you to bring your ass back with me for real, G. You remember how my dad and Uncle Jimmie used to run shit together, that's how I want it to be with us. I've already got connects from Pops. I have to fly out to the Dominican Republic to meet with this Dominican cat and I want you to fly out with me. I know I said I was thinking about retiring but that's after I get you used to all the connects, then I can just pass the shit to you."

"Say no more cuz, you know I'm down," Eazy replied.

When my pops passed away, he had already taught me how to run the streets and introduced me to all of his connects. He and my uncle ran New York together, my dad put him on and when dad passed and left it all to me, my uncle got on some snake shit and I haven't spoken to that nigga in years. I heard he was back in town and I have yet to pay his ass a visit. I looked up to my father and my uncle. He just turned his back on me and I can't get past that shit. Everything they did, they made sure I was a part of it to prepare me for the business. Taking trips overseas, setting up offshore accounts, there's nothing they didn't show me how to do. But now that I've got it, he wants to take it from me by any means. I just can't rock with shit like that. Family or not, I can't fuck with him.

I started this business as a youngster following behind my pops and Uncle. They hid nothing from me because they knew I would take on the business one day. At the age of thirteen, I caught my first body. I thought I would be nervous, but I did it and they even rewarded me when I finished.

"This is what happens when your workers double cross you," my dad said to me as he held the gun to his best friend Mike's head.

Yes, his best friend! No one is safe when it comes to you stealing drugs or money from my pops. My dad would give you the shirt off his back if he had too. His best friend started doing coke and that's a habit you just can't kick overnight. My dad noticed his shit was always short. Uncle Mike used to say it was another worker, and it even got the worker killed, until my dad walked into the warehouse and saw him practically putting a whole brick up his nose. He put him in rehab and he got out six months later trying to prove to my dad that he was a changed man. Once my dad saw him stealing money again he decided to follow him. We ended up at this vacant lot where my uncle bought a kilo from this white dude. My dad had me in the back seat and soon as the white guy pulled off. He waited to see if Unc would leave, but he didn't! He was sitting there snorting as much as he could at a time. We got out and walked over to his black Tahoe. Pops made him get out the car and stand at the edge of the bridge.

"I wanted to trust you, I gave you chance after chance and you still continued to steal from me. Well, I'm all out of chances." He looked at me and handed me his .45 after he put a silencer on it.

"Rock, look... it's me... Uncle Mikey! Don't do this!" Uncle Mike cried out to me but without hesitation, I pulled the trigger.

Pow! Pow!

My Uncle Mike fell into the river and we turned to walk away and got back in the truck.

"I'm proud of you son," my pops said.

After that, I became the "go get 'em" guy! Any problems my dad or Uncle Jimmie had, all they had to say was "Go Getem" and I was out the door, only to return hours later with a souvenir. After a kill, I would cut off a body part. I enjoyed snatching out their tongues if my pops said they snitched, I would cut off their hands if they stole anything from him, and burn out their eyes with a blow torch if pops said they saw something they weren't supposed to see.

I never told my cousin Eazy about that part of the business, he only thinks I dibble and dabble with drugs here and there and I plan to keep it like that, even when he decides to move with me. I know he would be more than willing to start working with me, but I can't lose him. He and Blaise are the only brothers I have.

"Aye, E, before you drop Rocko off, take me to the store I need to get something," Chino said.

We pulled up to the store, he gets out and I see this nigga at the register getting condoms. "You mean to tell me ole girl knows you coming over and ain't got the protection waiting for you?" I asked as he got back in the truck.

"Man, I don't trust shorty like that, she may stick a safety pin through my shit. I ain't fucking with her like that. She's good enough to fuck but not have my seed. The only way my fucking nut is going to touch her stomach is through her mouth. She found out she was pregnant a few weeks ago and went to the abortion clinic."

"Damn, you let that bitch have an abortion?" Blaise asked while rolling up another blunt.

"You fucking right I did, it wasn't my baby. She's got a dude she's been messing with besides me who pays for all of her shit and if his ass only knew I be knee deep in that pussy on a regular. That's why I make sure I bring my own shit with me. I ain't fucking her ass raw, my nigga."

Heading to my crib, I sent a text to this lil' shorty I fuck with to meet me at my crib. After that flight and fucking with these niggas all day, I need to release this pressure. As soon as I got out the shower, she was already at the door.

"What's up, shorty?" I said, opening the door as she jumped up and wrapped her legs around me. Damn, ma you couldn't wait to see daddy, huh?"

"Baby, you know I've been missing yo ass. You stayed away a little too long. You might as well just let me move in with you so you can have some in house pussy," she said as she started pulling my dick out my boxers.

"Who said I didn't? Shorty look, I've got a girl and you already know that. This ain't going no further than a fuck. You knew what it was before you signed up!" I grumbled.

She already knows what this is and it ain't ever been that. Bri already had five kids at twenty-six years old, so I'm good on that.

That lil' bitch is too fertile for me. Feeling the warmth of her mouth on my dick pulled me out of my thoughts. She knew exactly how I liked it. She sucked my dick so good it made a nigga's toes curl.

"Drop them, kids, off," she said while sucking my soul out my dick.

Feeling myself getting ready to explode, I grab her head and put my dick deep in the back of her throat and dropped my kids off like she asked. She swallowed every drop. She knew how that shit turned me on. Bri was bad as hell and kind of looked like Meagan Good. She just had too much shit going on to make her my woman. So I always made shit quick with her so she wouldn't catch feelings. I would nut and throw her ass out.

"Oh, I can't get the dick today?" Bri asked as she laid on the bed playing with her pussy.

"Nah, mama I've got a run to make, let's go!" I said, waving my hand, so she can follow me out the door.

I jumped in my Challenger doing the dash to my guy Wale crib while Kevin Gates bleed through my speakers

Do you think I'll ever need you love more than you need me?
Show me your true colors girl, I just want to see
Cause I done had too many come around and change up on
me
She screamin' please don't waste my time
I say I totally agree
See girl I'm fine with that
I done gave my watches away, ain't got no time for that

Askin' where's my heart, good luck findin' that

"What's good, Wale?" I asked, stepping into the house.

"Shit bruh, how long are you in town for?"

"Not long, you know I get my shit and dip back to my city."

"That's what's up, I've got some shit for you, though, wait right here let me get your bread out the back."

Wale was my guy and also one of my workers. It wasn't that I didn't trust Eazy doing it all, I just know Blaise like to be careless at times and I couldn't have all my shit getting taken by the police. After I finished chopping it up with him, I went to my girl Dorian's crib. Bri was just a bitch I would let suck my dick, but Dorian was the bitch I fucked with heavy. After hitting the block a minute, I headed her way.

Unlocking the door and putting my keys down on the kitchen table. I started walking to my bedroom down the hall. As soon as I got halfway there, I heard some moans coming out the room. I took my gun out my waist and kept walking down the hall. *I know damn well she doesn't have a nigga in my shit,* I said to myself as I reached the door. This nigga had my bitch bent over on my fucking bed. I started seeing red real quick.

"Bitch, I know you lost yo fucking mind!" She jumped up and ran to the corner. He turned around and pointed his gun back at me. That's when I noticed who he was. "What the fuck is yo ass doing here? Don't tell me this was the lil' bitch you were talking about earlier?" I asked still pointing my gun at him.

"Man, Rocko, I didn't know she was your girl," Chino said, lowering his gun and adjusting his pants.

"You're right, *was* my girl. BITCH, GET THE FUCK OUT MY SHIT right now!" I screamed.

"No, Rocko. Please, baby, I'm sorry I don't want him," she pleaded.

"Bitch, you still have my nut on yo chin, fuck is you talking bout?"! Chino yelled back at her.

"Rocko, baby, I will do anything to make this up to you. I can put him out right now and it can just be you and me!" she exclaimed.

"Nah, hoe. I know my way out I don't need nobody to escort me no got damn where."

"Dorian, I told yo ass once to get the fuck out my spot, so why the fuck are you still here?

"Rock, I don't have anywhere to go!" she screamed back, while trying to put her clothes on.

"Oh nah, you thought I meant put yo clothes on first? No, I meant to get the fuck out my shit now, as is! Bitch, you came here with nothing, so you leave with nothing."

As she walked past me to head out the door, I hit her in the face with the back of my gun, she dropped down to the floor crying. "Don't ever fucking disrespect me like that, and Chino you can get the fuck out too!" I yelled still holding my gun up at him just in case this nigga wanted to try me.

He knows I'm crazy as the fuck and that shit will go left real quick! I guarantee you I will be the only one walking out this bitch alive. "Say no more, I'm gone. Y'all can have this bullshit!" Chino spat with his hands up surrendering.

"I didn't know you knew him, Rocko!" she screamed from the floor, holding her mouth with blood hanging from her lips.

"So, you think if I caught you with someone I didn't know the shit will feel better? Bitch get the fuck on."

She turned to walk out the door then I remember that shit Chino said earlier. "Dorian come here," I called out to her as calm as possible.

"Thank you, baby I knew you would change your mind." She ran back to me.

"Earlier, Chino told me you were pregnant and you had an abortion." Her mouth dropped open like she was surprised, "So...you killed my baby? Ain't no way you thought I wouldn't take care of my seed, bitch, look at how I've got you living and you ain't even my fucking wife. You don't work, I take care of everything and this is what the fuck you do?!" I screamed.

"Baby, I'm sorry. You're barely here and I didn't want to raise the baby alone."

That blew the fuck out of me when she said that. The next thing I know, I grabbed her ass and started beating the fuck out of her. "First, you fuck a nigga in my crib, that was strike one, then you kill my fucking baby, now that shit took you right to strike three." I started choking the shit out of her. "Bitch, if my baby had to go then you have to go too, simple as that."

"Rocko, man, chill. You're about to kill this bitch."

After Chino pulled me off of her, she ran outside naked holding her neck and gasping for air. "Ok, yo ass can leave now too!" I yelled.

I kicked both of them out and called Bri over. I know her pussy was probably still dripping from earlier and the way I feel right now, I needed to knock the bottom out before I kill some damn body.

"Who is the bitch outside your door crying?' Bri asked as she walked in and quickly got undressed.

"Ma, that chick is the least of you worries. Now bring that ass here and make daddy feel good," I said while stroking my dick.

She kneeled down in front of me on the couch and started sucking my mans up like she was trying to see how many licks it took to get to the center. "Damn, ma!" I groaned as I started fucking her mouth faster. She didn't even flinch; she just took all that dick in her mouth and believe me when I say, my shit ain't small at all. She came up and tried to sit right on my dick, but I stopped her and reached for my rubber. That bitch knew I wasn't about to fuck her like that.

Pulling her ass down on my dick, I watched lil' mama go to work. Throwing her head back, she was riding my dick like she was on one of those fucking mechanical bulls or some shit. Bri had some good pussy, I couldn't deny her of that. I started gripping shorty by the waist and bouncing her up and down. I could feel her squeezing my dick with her pussy every time she bounced up. I wasn't ready to nut yet so I came out of the pussy for a second and turned her ass around then started digging in that pussy again. With one leg on the couch and one behind my head, I was on my *Paid In Full* Dougie shit.

"Yes, Rock right there! Hmmm... yesss daddy, hmmm... hmmm... fuck baby shit," she moaned as she pulled me closer to her from the back.

"Take this dick, girl," I said as I pounded her harder, taking all my frustration out on her.

She started throwing it back harder and faster and my nut instantly started filling up the condom. As soon as I came, she turned around and started sucking my dick with the condom still on. Now, I done been with some freaks, but nobody could top Bri. Now I see why her ass got so many damn kids running around here.

I went to the bathroom and turned on my shower. I needed that shit cause Dorian and Chino's bitch ass had me fucked up. That's why I don't trust these hoes now. No matter how good you are to them, they will still fuck another nigga. I'm convinced that they are all the same. So, like Uncle Snoop said, "We don't love them hoes."

"I'm about to jump in the shower so I can go to bed, I'll holla at you tomorrow," I told Bri when I noticed her headed to the shower too.

"Rocko, it's two a.m., I can't stay? She asked.

"Hell no. Don't you have a four-month-old at home? And from the way that milk dripping out your breasts, you might want to take yo ass on home and feed his lil' ass, now get the fuck out so I can go to sleep unless you want to be like shorty on the steps." She grabbed her things and quickly left.

Chapter 5

Eazy

"Man, I've got the munchies, what's in the fridge?" I asked.

"Not a damn thing, we've gotta grab something to eat after this shit, E." he replied.

Rolling up a blunt, I kicked my feet up on the table and admired how this shit is decked out with glass tables and shit. It was real high class. "Yo, I forgot to tell you about my night," Rocko said.

"What happened, did you meet up with ole girl?"

"Yea, man listen! So I go to my crib where I let shorty stay at. I walk in the damn house and go back to the bedroom where I thought shorty was at right. I get half way down the hall, and I hear this bitch moaning."

"Don't tell me, she was in there watching Porn Hub?" I laughed

"Nigga, no. So I pulled my gun out, I get to the door and this bitch in there sucking off another nigga in my shit, E!

"Noooo. I know there ain't no fucking way you let that shit slide. Where you hide the bodies? Cause I know you fucked both of them up? I asked.

"Nah, I choked the shit out of her ass though and kicked her the fuck out naked. That ain't the bad part tho, Eazy. The nigga she was fucking was yo boy!" Rocko said.

"My boy? Man, unless it was Blaise or Chino, you know I don't fuck with nobody else."

"Right, it was yo boy Chino."

"Now I know you already half way fuck with this nigga, so I know you unloaded on his ass."

"Nah, you know I don't sweat the small stuff, but after I remembered the shit he said earlier about her having an abortion that's when I went crazy on her ass and he had to pull me up off her..." I was interrupted by laughter approaching and keys opening the door.

"Cocoa, what I tell you about smoking in the fucking house? Just cause yo dumb ass raise the window doesn't mean the damn scent goes away! Karma spat, "Sis, I been with you all day, what the hell are you talking about?" she replied, walking into the kitchen to put the groceries down.

"I'm glad y'all hoes brought food home, cause we got tired of sitting here hungry."

She dropped the food on the floor as she jumped from seeing Rocko and I sitting at the kitchen table. "Instead of stealing my money, yo ass should have been stealing some fucking groceries! How yo place gone be this dope, but you ain't got no food, ma?" I asked.

"How did you get in my shit?" Cherish inquired.

"You want to know how I got in and I want to know how you stole my shit in front of my face. Now, you go first!!" I said, pulling out my .9mm and pointing it at her head. "Now, I'm only going to ask you one more time, where is my money?"

"I told yo ass he was gone find you," Cocoa said as she took a seat next to me.

"Don't you try to act like this shit is sweet, bitch. You lied like her ass and said she didn't stay here!" I spat.

"Aye, at the end of the day that's my sister, I wasn't about to let you hurt her. But you here now, so what's up?"

"Bitch, I want my fucking money back, that's what's up!" I threatened as she sat down like she didn't know what I was talking about.

"Don't give me that damn look, yo ass remember me from the other morning in the store."

"Oh yea, the guy with all the women, so did they like the outfits?

"Don't try to twist this shit. What did you do to my damn card?" I said while walking closer to her on the couch.

"Just tell him CeCe, so he can leave."

"And who the fuck are you?" I asked, looking at the girl who almost looks just like Cherish. "I'm Karma, her sister, and I just want her to be honest so you can take yo ass on!" she yelled back at me.

"Oh, even if she was being honest, I ain't going nowhere until I get my money. Point blank period, so y'all might as well make room for me and my guy here," I said pointing over at Rocko. He went back into the kitchen and started making a damn sandwich, "Aye, where's the red Kool-Aid at?" he yelled from the kitchen.

"We don't drink Kool-Aid!" Karma yelled out in a tone that she should surely lower.

"How y'all black with no Kool-Aid?" he asked.

"Look, let's get back to business, where's my money?"

"I don't have it," Cherish replied.

"Yo ass needs to go and get it," I said while putting my gun on my lap.

"Good luck with that, because my ass doesn't have a job anymore, so you might as well count that change as a loss," she said while folding up here arms.

Before I knew it, I jumped up and smacked her ass. "Don't tell me what to count my fucking money as and since you can't get my money than yo ass gone work for me, how about that? Since you ain't got no job looks like you ain't got shit else to do in this bitch!" I saw shorty moving slowing to the side of the couch while I was talking to Cherish and the next thing I know, she pulled a purple Beretta out and pointed that shit at me.

"Karma, sis just put it down, we will get out of this. PLEASE JUST PUT THE GUN DOWN!" Cherish yelled out to her.

"Oh, you want to shoot me for your sister stealing my shit? You got this shit all backwards, ma." Rocko came from out the kitchen after hearing Cherish mentioned lowering a gun.

"Now, bitch unless you have a death wish you might want to put that down," Rocko said while putting the red beam right in the middle of her forehead from where he was standing. "Play with it if you want to, I'm not Eazy. If you steal from me, I'll steal back; the only difference is I'm stealing your soul like I'm Grim Reaper and you can't get that shit back. Now, put that gun down and join the conversation like he said!" Rocko yelled while taking another bite of his sandwich.

"What do I have to do?" CeCe asked.

"We will discuss that in the truck."

"The truck? I ain't going nowhere with you," she said through clenched teeth

"Oh, you wanna bet?" Rocko said while standing up and pulling her off the couch. "Go get yo ass in the truck, and y'all bitches better not fucking move," he said while pointing the gun at them.

I figured since my little brother like to keep shit at the house, I'll have her ass stay there and work, versus having those other hoes there.

"Where are you taking me?" she asked, I ignored her cause she will see soon enough where she will be spending the next few months until her debt is paid.

Pulling up to my brother's crib, I took her in around the back. "Aye, Blaise, I've got something for you," I said as I came from down the hall.

He had one girl in the kitchen and the other one, he was fucking the shit out of in the living room. Chino ass was sitting across the room watching TV like this nigga ain't in here fucking a bitch.

"Say bruh, I see you found that black bitch," Blaise said while letting his eyes roll to the back of his head. I see this man had no problem with having an audience.

"You might want to go ahead and wrap that shit up, cause I don't have all day," I said as I shook my head at him. He stepped back like he was about to stop but rammed his dick back inside her.

"Go ahead and talk, I'm listening!" Blaise said.

"I brought you a house guest." Blaise instantly stopped fucking shorty.

"Wait, man, what you mean? Timeout, flag on the play, offsides, now run that shit by me again," he said.

"Nigga, this ain't no damn football," I said, laughing out loud at his goofy ass. "Before I go into more details, shorty has gotta go for real."

"Aight, she can go soon as y'all step into the kitchen for a minute," Blaise said while turning ole girl around and making her get on her knees.

The next thing I hear is his ass screaming "Ooooohhhhhh... shit, ma. Ok, now you can go, my brother and I have business to discuss."

"Aight, y'all can come back in now!" Blaise yelled from the living room.

"I'm making shorty work with you. Since you like to stay at home, I figured you needed the company."

"Bruh is this not the same girl who not only stole white folks eye color, but she stole your money too? What makes you so sure she wouldn't do it again? I don't know about you, but I'm not trying to come home to an empty ass house."

"Her ass sees how far I'll go to find her but this time, she won't come back alive if she keeps fucking with me. So Cherish, anything my brother needs you to do, you need to do it and in an orderly fashion. From cooking, cleaning, baking cakes…"

"Sucking my dick," Blaise added.

"Except sucking his dick," I said. I mean if you do, that's on you but just know that's not gone help you pay off your debt for me. Anyway, she'll be here a few months. Wherever he goes, you will be two steps behind him. He will never leave you unsupervised and no this is not a kidnapping, yo ass just can't go nowhere unless it's with Blaise or myself. You got that?"

"It sounds like a fucking kidnapping to me," she mumbled.

"Excuse me! Speak up, I didn't catch that," I replied, knowing I heard exactly what's she said. I just wanted her to repeat it again so I could hit her ass.

"Nothing, I didn't say anything. Will I at least be able to talk to my sisters?"

"Only when I take you home to get more clothes, then it's back to work you go. And don't take this shit out on me because this is the ditch that you dug for yourself. Now come on let me show you to your room."

My brother has a four bedroom three and a half bathroom crib, so he has more than enough space for shorty to stay. Her ass really doesn't deserve to live this well after stealing my shit. I walked her into the room and showed her where the bathroom was located inside of the room. I watched her as she walked to the bathroom and turned the lights on like she was trying to see if she would have to flush the toilet with her foot. You know how women do when they go to public bathrooms.

"Here's my number, only use it for emergencies only. Other than that, ask Blaise. I'm about to bounce, y'all enjoy," I said as I walked out the room only to be met by my brother Blaise.

"I know what you trying to do but it won't work," he said.

"Yea, I'm trying to make her work my money off, what you thought?" I asked Blaise.

"Nah, you're trying to get me to settle down and wife shorty's fine ass up. She may be a thief, but I bet her ass is freaky as hell too. That's my type of woman," Blaise said while rubbing his hands together like Birdman.

"I may be a freak but you will never know it," Cherish said as she came from the back room.

"So you're saying I can't slide up in that thang tonight?"

"Yea, it's this little thing called palm of."

"Bitch, what the hell is palm of?" Blaise asked with a curious look on his face. I laughed cause I know he wasn't about to fall for this shit.

"Nigga, the palm of yo hand, and watch that bitch word!" she replied and walked back down the hallway.

I was dying laughing. My brother thought just cause he was fly every bitch wanted to fuck him, but it looks like this one will be a challenge. I would be scared to stick my dick in this one, though, not cause she's nasty but cause she may steal that bitch too.

"Man, I really hope this shit work out, because I'd hate to kill this bitch if she steals anything else."

Chapter 6

CeCe

Waking up in a home that's not mine feels weird as hell. I don't know how I got myself caught up in some shit like this. I would only have to worry about myself if my sisters weren't so damn lazy or doing freaky shit for money. Looking around the room, they do have this fit for a queen, though. It had nice 55-inch TV on the wall, a queen size bed, nice fluffy pillows and most importantly, satin pillow cases for my natural hair.

"Get up lil' mama, I need help in here!" Blaise yelled through the door.

Fuck, this is going to be a long day. I came out the room only to see scales, bags, some kind of sharp cutter thing and face mask.

"Come sit here, let me show you how this shit goes," Blaise insisted.

I must have sat there for hours watching him break down, weigh and bag shit up. He repeated the process so many times to me I began to dose off. Every time I woke up, this nigga was still talking. Like fuck, does the boy ever hush?

"Ok, we have been at this for hours now and I haven't eaten anything. I'm sure I can do this shit backwards now, as many times as you showed it to me. I am about to cook some lunch or something, then we can get back to this," I stated, getting up off the couch and going into the kitchen. I opened the fridge to see this nigga ain't got shit in here.

"Umm, do you want to take me to the store? Because apparently, you haven't been in months," I requested.

"Yea, I'll take you. Put some clothes on and let me put this stuff away."

We rode to Walmart in silence; it's almost like he is afraid to talk to me. "Blaise, is it?" I asked, trying to break the tension between us.

"Yea, it's Blaise," he replied, being very short with me.

"I'm sure your mother didn't name you that, what's your real name?"

"What's up with all the police ass questions? What are you trying to steal now, my identity like you stole my brother's money?" he said as he looked at me with what looked like fire in his eyes.

"Hell no, I was trying to make conversation with yo ass. I'm doing whatever I have to do to pay your brother back. So you don't have to throw that shit in my face every day.

"What made you do that shit anyway?" he questioned.

I really hate to tell this story over and over again, so here it goes.

"I started stealing people's credit card information when I ran across this new device they have out where you can use your phone to swipe the card. I had this nerdy ass man that liked me to rig it up so that one swipe will erase their entire account and it would go to an anonymous account of mine that's completely untraceable. They would be able to search so far but will always end up at the dead in. At first, I started doing it to make sure my sisters and I were good, and I would regret it after I did it but now, I do it with no hesitation and not even an ounce of remorse. It worked for me for over three years now until that day your brother came in. When you guys walked up to the doors, all I saw was money dripping off him."

He had on this black Movado watch and Brunello Cucinelli jeans that I know cost damn near $800. He had the whitest teeth I had ever seen. When he smiled, I could have sworn I saw a reflection of an angel through his teeth. Just thinking about his ass and telling this story has me blushing. This man was some type of fine and I never expected to see him again.

"That day he showed up at my house spooked me, but I thought Cocoa got rid of them until I came home and his ass was sitting in my kitchen. So, now I'm here!"

"Damn, so where are you parents?" he asked.

"I have no damn clue where my mom is and I've never met my dad. All I know is he and my mom dated a while before I was born. I don't know his name and I don't know if he is dead or alive. It's just my sisters and me."

I wasn't expecting any sympathy after that story, but I could look at Blaise and tell it kind of got to him. Every time I tell it, I get a little relief from all the pain and pressure I have built up. For three years I've been playing super sister asking if Karma is ok, if Cocoa is ok, but no one ever asks CeCe if she's ok. The truth is, I'm not! I'm tired of all this shit and I just want to live my life for me. I'm twenty-five years old and I feel like I'm a single parent who's tied down with two kids. I don't want to feel like this for the rest of my life.

We pulled up to Walmart and I could tell the tension had eased up a little bit after our talk. He was talking way more than he was at first.

"What's your favorite meal?" I asked.

"I haven't had a good home cooked meal in a minute."

"Ok, what do you have in mind then?"

"For lunch, I want Sloppy Joe and curly fries and for dinner, I want dressing, ham, macaroni and cheese, green beans, oh and some yams!" he rambled

I really regret asking his ass that now. I've never cooked dressing in my life. Don't look at me funny either; y'all know my mama is a crackhead, so the last thing on her mind was teaching her daughters how to cook. Hell, I had to read the back of my Always pads to see how to use them. That shows you how much she wasn't around to teach us girly shit. Good thing I have my Pinterest app on my phone, I'm sure someone has a good recipe on there. I'll just fake it till I make it.

"Ok cool, I can make that happen for you." *Oh Lord please let this shit, I mean stuff, turn out good,* I thought to myself.

After he paid for all of the groceries, we headed back towards the house. He started back breaking stuff down and bagging it up, while I cooked up a small lunch and started preparing my cornbread for the dressing I was cooking later. After lunch, Blaise started rolling a blunt. I don't smoke, so I just went back into the guest room. Whatever he in there smoking is loud as hell.

Knock! Knock!

"You wanna hit?" Blaise asked as soon as I opened the door.

"I'd rather not," I replied, waving the smoke out of my face.

"It's not like you got a job to go to, it's Friday, stimulate yo mind!" he joked.

"Ha ha boy, you are not Smokey. I guess one hit wouldn't hurt."

One hit turned into five. Why didn't anyone tell me Kush was so damn good? That shit had me high as hell! I could have sworn I saw Edris Elba lying next to me asshole naked but when I reached over to touch him, my hand was pushed away.

"Cherish, what the hell are you grabbing on my dick for?" Eazy yelled out. "Keep playing and I'ma put this big boy in yo life," he said, causing Blaise to bust out laughing. I guess in the midst of us smoking, I fell asleep and Eazy came back over.

"My bad, I was not trying to touch you."

"It's cool, I may not like yo ass but my dick doesn't discriminate at all."

I just got up and went into the kitchen and started getting dinner ready. I didn't want to say the wrong thing to him nor do the wrong thing to him because I'm high and horny. I don't even know if that's a good combination or not, I do know he better leave me alone before I rape his fine ass.

Hours later the food was done; Blaise and I tore that damn food up. That dressing was on point, so thanks to whoever posted it on Pinterest. After dinner, we watched the *Conjuring 2* and it had both of our asses wanting to sleep in the living room with the lights on. Watching movies became our nightly thing. We would wake up, I cook us breakfast, pretend to watch him break shit down, cook lunch, dinner, smoke and watch movies.

"You are cooler than I thought you would be," Blaise said while we were eating another one of his favorite meals— neck bones, macaroni and cheese, greens and cornbread.

This man was an old person at heart. My sisters and I barely ate shit like this, we would always get something quick to pop in the microwave or I would try to meal prep and that shit always failed. I just stuck with making smoothies every morning until I came here. I know I've gained about five pounds since being here and it all went right to my ass. I can't even front like I didn't like it. My body started looking like Fantasia's; her body is thick as hell, the only thing is I have a little more booty than she does.

"You're not so bad yourself!" I replied, "I thought I would hate it here but after getting to know you, I feel more comfortable being here. Don't get me wrong, I most definitely miss my own bed, but I've fallen in love with that pillow top in that room, that bitch be having me in a coma." We both laughed, finished dinner and got ready for bed.

Chapter 7

Cocoa

Every morning I wake up it's a bundle of roses on my doorstep addressed to me. It's really starting to freak me out because it doesn't say who they are from. I would just toss them in the dumpster on the way out only for more flowers to be at my door again. With this shit going on I may need to change my career. Yes, I feel like my job is a career, don't judge me and yes, I called it a job. I work eight hours just like you and I take my lunch break just like you. I've got a hoe-01K, just like you have a 401K. The only thing now is the pussy is too good and these men are apparently starting to become stalkers and I can't have that shit.

"Karma, I'm headed out for a little while. I left money on the kitchen table for you to do whatever with today!" I yelled as I walked to the door.

"Thanks, Cocoa, I guess I'll get out this house today. I'm starting to get bored as hell just waiting on CeCe to come home."

"She'll be home eventually. I'm gone, spend that money wisely," I replied waving goodbye as I walked down the stairs. She's going to flip when she see it's a stack on the kitchen table. All I know she had better buy me a thank-you gift.

Jumping into my rental car, I did the dash to Dr. King's office. Lately, I've been seeing him every Tuesday and we didn't do much talking about my life anymore. Most days we would just have sex all around his office, he would eat my pussy until I fell asleep, or he would go on and on about how crazy he is about me and plan on leaving his wife. I always stop him in mid-sentence because Chloe Chanel Carter does not plan on being anyone housewife. I like making my own money and in the manner I'm making it. I love fucking for a buck and doing something strange for a piece of change. I don't get a piece of change, though; I sell my pussy for $2,000 or greater. You have to be a boss to fuck with me, that's about the only thing mama did teach me.

Walking into his office, I see roses all over the room, candles and a blow-up mattress. This lil' white man had really lost his damn mind.

"I see your wife is coming, so I'll just leave," I stated as I started walking towards the door.

"No Chloe, this is all for you, I love you and I wanted to show you just how much I care about you."

"Wait... you what? I don't know what you thought but I don't love you and if you're about to get all weird on me, this shit is about to stop!" I spat.

This man has really lost it. I don't settle down and if I did it wouldn't be with him. I mean the dick is good and all, but not that damn good. I have a business to run and I can't do that shit tied down to his ass. So I did the only thing a sane person would do, I grabbed some of the covered strawberries and ran like hell. Don't judge me, I had to get away from him but not before I tasted those Berries that Pajae made; they were infused with liquor and I had to try them. His ass will be ok, he has a whole wife and kids at home that he needs to be spending time with and not trying to divorce his wife for me, especially since I don't want his ass at all.

Headed to the mall to grab a few things, I quickly jumped out the car and went towards Charlotte Russe. They had this cute camouflage jacket I just had to get. Looking in one direction, I ran slap dead into a wall— well it seemed like a wall.

"You might want to watch where you are going, shorty," Rocko said, as he reached down to help me off the ground.

"Yea, sorry about that, it's Rocko, right? I asked like I didn't remember the first day I saw him at my crib. He was fine then and looks even better now.

"Yea it's Rocko, but you can call me daddy," he said with a cute ass look on his face that had my ass in a trance.

"Well, I'm sorry I bumped into you, I was in a rush and looking one way. I'll let you get back to whatever you were doing." I smiled at him and walked away only to be pulled back by my waist.

"Wait ma, what are you running away for? Let me buy you lunch." He asked and staring at him there was no way in hell I could say no.

"I'll say yes if you can tell me how my sister is doing first," I replied stepping back and folding my arms.

"She's still alive as far as I know, so she's good!"

"Don't play, what you mean as far as you know?" I asked.

"Look shorty, she's good, now let's go grab something to eat."

"Wait, right here, let me go grab this coat and I'll be right back."

I turned to walk away, I plan on taking my time and if he's still there when I get back, I just may take him up on that offer. I must have walked around the mall five times going in and out of stores just to waste time. I tired my damn self out. I got my coat I was looking for so I started heading to my car. I was damn near out the door and I heard someone calling out.

"Say shorty, you had me sitting here for almost an hour, and then you try to walk past me like you didn't see me sitting here. You're lucky I didn't have shit else to do or I would've left," he said, knowing damn well he didn't want to leave.

"You could have left but now that we are both here, let's go."

We walked out to his truck and he sped off. I couldn't help but stare at his ass, my pussy was jumping, I'm horny as hell and Dr. King came with that bullshit today. I could have had some good meat.

"Where are we going?" I asked.

"To my favorite restaurant called Another Broken Egg, they have some good shit in there."

"Sounds good, I'm not that hungry but I can eat," I replied.

"I've been having my eyes on your smart mouth ass since I first met you. You blew me off though, so I took that L like a man and left. I see you were feeling the kid tho."

"Whatever, what made you think that?"

"Well, either you are feeling me or yo ass just wanted a free meal. You know how you females do. A nigga can be ugly as hell and she will still go as long as he's paying." We laughed together because that right there was the truth.

"Nah you're aight, I guess. I can buy my own food and yours, so the free food has nothing to do with it."

"That's what's up, I love it when a woman has her own. That only gives me more reasons to spoil her. You look like the type that likes to be spoiled."

"I look like the type who can spoil a nigga if I wanted to. Before you start thinking I'm a gold digger, I've got money so trust me, I'm not sitting around waiting on a man to spoil me!" I spat, knowing damn well I was lying through my teeth.

"Pipe down shorty, I didn't say all that. And if you were my lady, I wouldn't let you spend a dime of your money cause it would be my job to make sure you are taken care of."

"Yea I guess. Anyway, are we almost there because I'm getting hungry now and the way you are talking I can buy up the menu." I started laughing and continued to look out the window.

We pulled up to the restaurant and he came around and opened the door for me to help me out of his truck. I had on my dark denim Fashion Nova jeans, a white body shirt, and some Jessica Simpson's pumps.

I could tell he was watching my ass as we went inside the restaurant. "If you take a picture, it would last longer." I chuckled.

"What you talking about?"

"You're looking at my ass. Nigga, I see yo ass," I let out flirtatiously.

We sat down, talked, and laughed for a minute and left the restaurant. We headed to a bar after that and had a few more drinks. I wanted him in the worse way, my pussy was throbbing for him. I don't know if it was the drinks or what, but I need this man inside of me. I can imagine him pinning my short thick ass to a wall, wrapping my legs around him and he just starts beating my guts out.

"Say shorty, we're back at your car. You dosed off after we left the bar. If you think you had too much to drink, I can take you home."

"No, I'm ok thanks for everything, though, I really enjoyed myself."

"Same here shorty, I'll see you later. Plug my number in your phone first," he said and called out his number.

Well, good thing I bought some of that Bedroom Kandi Javolco sold me or as bad as I would hate that, I would have to make a trip to see Dr. King. Rocko ass just drove off and left me with a wet pussy and leftovers in my hand.

Chapter 8

Rocko

As I drove away from her, I couldn't help but think about the brief time we spent together. The front she put on of her being a tough girl made me want to know what makes her act like that. She's beautiful as hell, her deep dimples pop every time she starts to talk. I decided to turn around and see if I could catch her before she pulled off. I wasn't ready to end yet.

Hitting a U-turn in the middle of the street, I quickly made my way back to the parking lot where I dropped her off. She was sitting inside the car on the phone. I got out and tapped on her window.

"Come and take a ride with me?" I asked as she let her window down.

"For what? Where we going?" she questioned, like I was gone do something to her ass.

"I just want to kick it a little more and talk, that's it."

"Let me call you later," she said and hung up the phone. She got out the car and walked over to my truck and got in. After I got back in the truck we drove off and rode until I saw a park.

"I wasn't ready to end things with you. I'm not trying to sound weird or some shit but I just want to know more about you. I can't lie like I'm not intrigued. It's something about you that's drawing me to you. My ass is usually not so quick to want to know someone, but this shit just feels different."

"It's cool. I don't mind spending more time with you, is not like my ass had something to do anyway. Cherish is still gone and Karma is probably reading a book, she's obsessed with that new author Shaniya Denise."

She laid her seat back, opened my sunroof and kicked her feet up like she was at home. I had to laugh on the inside. Normally, I would curse a bitch out for putting their feet on my dashboard but I'll let her slide.

"So, tell me something that no one knows about you?" I asked.

"Like what's my favorite color?"

"Hell no, what's your darkest secret?"

"I'd rather keep that to myself. I don't think you are ready to hear that and plus, I have a psychiatrist if I wanted to talk about my darkest secret." She turned and started looking up through the sunroof. I loved the way the moon had her eyes sparkle a little.

"I'm sorry I wasn't trying to invade your privacy, I just wanted to know why you have this guard up like you scared to let someone in. I'm just gone be real honest with you. I don't want you to feel any type of way when I say this, but I just want to hear your side."

"You're getting serious on me, let me raise my damn seat up just in case you say the wrong thing," she replied.

"I'm not trying to disrespect you, but I did hear a few things about you and I can't say they were all good. The word on the street is that you sell yourself to the highest bidder. I don't mean any disrespect like I said before, I just wanted to know if it was true." I could see the rage pouring through her eyes and she damn near wanted to cut my damn throat. She sat up in her seat more and just started looking at me.

"Why are you asking me this shit?" she questioned.

"I told you, I wanted to get to know you more."

"So you wanted to see if I fuck for money, so you can fuck me? Is that why you brought me to this damn dark ass park, to fuck?"

"Chill, ma that's not why you are here, a nigga really wanted to talk and get to know you. I don't pay for pussy, never have and never will. I'm sorry if showing interest is something you're not used to but I'm not that nigga that just wants to fuck. If you don't feel comfortable, I can let you out and I'm sure an Uber is real close to pick you up. I would even wait till they arrive. But what you not gone do is try to show out on me like I'm one of those lame ass niggas you fuck with. You ain't never met a nigga like me. Now, do you want to go home or what? Cause I can find somebody else to spend my time with." I spat.

She's really got me fucked up thinking I wanted to buy pussy. Bitch, who the fuck do I look like? I can get any bitch I want but I wanted her. I saw her let her seat back and prop her feet back up.

"Since you want to know Chloe, then I'll tell you all about me and I'll give you the choice to leave or stay." She paused for a moment, then started letting it all out.

"When I was twelve years old, my mom started waking me up out my sleep because she had just sold me for a piece of crack," she said in an embarrassed tone. I didn't say anything, I just continued to listen.

"I didn't have a choice in losing my virginity because that shit was snatched away from me. She gave us the birds and the bees talk once we started our cycles and of course, this was before she got on drugs heavy. She told us how sacred our virginity was and how saving ourselves until marriage was not a bad thing. Our husband would respect us more by having a body that was pure and not tainted. But when she got on that shit, she could give a fuck about us. At twelve years old, I lost my virginity in a damn abandoned building. I loved my mama and even though I knew that shit was wrong, I also knew I couldn't tell her no. By the age of fifteen, I had become a sex addict. I loved having sex anywhere, any time of the day and I didn't care who was watching. It became something that I looked forward to doing several times a day and on top of that, I was making crazy money for it. My mom ran out on us when I was eighteen years old, I don't know where or who my dad is. It's just my sisters and I and we rarely get along. Cherish doesn't like the things I do, but I can't help it. As bad as I would love to stop and be with one person, no one will ever want to be with me how I want to be with them. My mom taught us that our pussy was powerful, we are walking ATMs as she says and no one can get something out without putting something in. You have to pay to play and I lived by that."

She finally took a deep breath and the tears started to fill up in her eyes. She probably looked at herself as a nasty woman, but in that moment I actually saw someone who was crying out to be loved correctly.

"You don't have to say anymore. I'm sorry if I opened up a box you weren't ready to reveal, but I'm glad you did. You said your story would make men run the other way basically. I'm telling you now that's not going to happen with me. If this is something you really want to stop doing then I've got your back 100%. No one has taken the time to love you properly and fucking with me, you wouldn't want to go back to that life anyway. My lifestyle may be a little bad but I'm a good dude. I've been hurt before, and it's hard for me to trust people. I'm willing to help you love yourself again, and I hope you can be here to help me trust again. I don't want you to change your ways for me, I want you to change them for yourself. You have to want this, so you have to love yourself more than you love sex," I explained.

The more I talked the more tears start to pour from her eyes. I leaned over, pulled her into my chest and just gave her that hug she has been needing for years. After talking for a few more hours we finally decided to take it in. She started getting sleepy and I have an early flight out.

We got back on the expressway and headed to her car.

"I leave in the morning but I'll be back, so make sure you make time for me. If you need to talk don't hesitate to call me no matter what time it is. I want to be here for you, but I can only be here if you let me." She nodded her head, I gave her a kiss on the forehead and helped her into her car. I got back into my truck and did the dash all the way home.

Chapter 9

Ce-Ce

Three months later

I've been working for Eazy a while now and sometimes it doesn't even feel like work. When I'm with Blaise it feels more like I'm with the little brother I've never had, but when Eazy comes over the whole vibe changes. It's like he wants people to not fuck with me because this was and still is all about business. I can't just sit when he's here, I'm constantly pretending like I have things to do. He supposed to come by today so I can go home and see my sisters. When we are in the truck, it's always dead silence and he has his radio up so loud to make sure if I did say something, he wouldn't hear me.

"Good morning Eazy, can I get you anything?" I asked as he entered the house.

"If I need something, I'll let you know. Now get dressed so I can drop you off."

I am so excited to see my sisters I'm not even going to let him kill my vibe right now. "Blaise, how has shorty been doing around here?" I heard Eazy ask.

"She has actually been good. I live the life of a king around this bitch; she cooks, cleans and helps me break the cakes down. Hell, the bitch even mowed the lawn and that's without me asking. The only thing she doesn't do is fuck me. She's trying to work this debt off fast so she can get back to her life."

I started slowly walking down the hall to continue eavesdropping, hoping he would say when I could go home for good. Even though I kind of like being here, I still miss my sisters. Surprisingly, I miss Cocoa too. Her smart ass mouth is what I miss most.

"I'm ready." I stepped out in my white and black striped spaghetti strap maxi dress that hugged my hips, with a big floppy black hat that held my big curly hair down. It's the middle of July and I was trying to be as cool as possible.

"Damn sis, you're looking good," Blaise said as I stepped into the room. He always called me sis, like I said, being here doesn't feel like work.

"Sis? Oh y'all cool like that, now?" Eazy asked.

"Man, she's been here over three months. There ain't no way we're supposed to sit here and not say shit to each other. She's cool people, I no longer think she just the black bitch with green eyes, that's sis for real, E. Shorty was trying to provide for her sisters so I can't even knock her for that, cause you would do the same for me."

I smiled at Blaise for taking up for me, I still don't think Eazy was feeling that shit at all, but, fuck him. This shit should all be over soon and I wouldn't give a damn if I saw his ugly ass anymore.

He wasn't really ugly, though, he's actually like the perfect mixtures of your favorite food. I think we would go so well together. Like greens and cornbread, neck bones and hot sauce, Kool-Aid with a ton of sugar the way that lil' boy mixed it in *House Party*. He was maybe 5'11, caramel skin tone, tattoos everywhere, tight sexy eyes and pretty ass teeth. My heart always speeds up when he entered the room. The way he looks at me, though, I know he is totally turned off from me. I was only trying to make sure my sisters were good. So I've been stuck here waiting on Blaise hand and foot. At first, I dreaded waking up in the mornings, but now it feels normal to me.

"Let's go," Eazy said, pulling me from my thoughts. We got into his Charger and he blasted "Scarpe" a song off Future's latest CD the entire way.

"Do you mind stopping by Wendy's so I can grab a 4 for $4? I haven't eaten anything all day and a bitch is hungry as hell."

"Yea, I mind! You don't need to be eating that bullshit; that shit goes right to your ass," he said. And as he could see I've been eating this shit a minute because all I have is ass and I like that, so this nigga better pull the hell up to this drive-thru and quit playing with me.

As we took the exit to Popular Avenue, he pulled into Newks and parked. *I know he is not serious,* I said to myself. *This does not look like a burger joint to me.*

"You must be about to get something from here, right?" I asked.

"Nope, you are, I'm not letting you put those fake ass frozen patties in your body while you are around me, now get your ass out and get that grilled chicken salad with light ranch dressing."

Ok, I know he must be joking, so I continued to sit there and wait on him to pull off. We must have sat there damn near thirty mins and he was still sitting there on his phone. He was dead ass serious about me not getting a burger. I got out and ordered my grilled chicken salad with light ranch dressing and as soon as I got back in the truck, he pulled off. *Ain't this about a bitch,* I said to myself. A few moments later we pulled up to the house.

"I'll be back in two hours, so be ready," he said as he pulled off leaving skid marks in the street.

"Honey, I'm home!" I screamed as I entered the house.

"Sisssssss!" Karma screamed as she ran up to me. I've been missing you so much, his ass needs to bring you by here more than once a damn week."

"Girl, I know but this will be all over soon baby. Where's Cocoa?" I asked as I looked into the rooms and saw Karma was home alone.

"She said she had another appointment today, she's usually home all day with me since you haven't been home. She has been paying some of the bills around here and giving me money too," Karma said.

"What do you mean some? What about the rest of them? See, that's that bullshit! I didn't pick and choose the bills I paid. I just paid them all and she wants to pick the small ass light bill or cable bill and leave the fucking $750 rent for me!" I spat.

"She didn't pick the bills sis, that's just all he left for her to pay. He has been coming by here every month since you have been gone and leaving the rent money on the table. I'm still not even sure how he got inside the house and the only way I knew who it was is because I was coming home one day as he was walking out. Karma stated.

"Who is this he, Karma?" I asked.

"Eazy," she replied.

"Eazy, are you sure?" I asked with the look of confusion on my face.

"Yes, I'm sure. I can't forget the face that scared the shit out of me sitting in my damn kitchen. You didn't know he was coming by here?" she asked.

"No sis, I didn't know.

I assumed Cocoa was keeping up with everything, so I never bothered asking and he never mentioned anything to me. But, why would he do that if I owe him money? That's him losing more money. I'm not sure what's going on now. If I'm not there paying my debt off to him, why in the fuck does he still have me cooped up in Blaise fucking house like this? Now, I can't wait till he picks me up so I can see what is going on and when I can take my ass home.

After finishing up my salad, I laid across the couch and waited on Eazy to pull back up. I must have dosed off because I didn't wake up until I heard Cocoa coming through the door laughing loudly.

"What's up Cherish? I see they finally let yo ass out of solitary confinement," Cocoa said as she entered the house with a gentleman behind her.

"Yea, they did, but what do you think you're about to do? You know the rules, no men in the house."

She proceeds to walk into the bedroom. "Sorry sis, that rule was broken when two guys came looking for yo ass. Besides, you don't pay bills here anymore so whatever I want to do, I can do. Unless Eazy tells me not to since he is the one paying the rent and shit now. I guess you finally started using what you got to get what you want!" Cocoa spat.

"And what is that supposed to mean?" I asked as I followed them into her bedroom.

"Don't you see I'm busy here? We will talk when I'm done. Now close my fucking door."

I had just about enough of Cocoa. I don't give a fuck who pay the bills, my name is on all this shit. I heard her lock the door, so I pulled my dress up by my thighs and kicked that bitch in.

"Cherish, stop fucking with me.

"I said his ass can't be in here! This is my shit regardless of what the fuck you think. Take that thot shit somewhere else or we about to go toe-to-toe in this bitch and you know I ain't never took an L!" I screeched. He looked at me and grabbed his shit and got the fuck out.

"Now, if you have a problem with the way I run MY SHIT, go get YO SHIT and you can fuck in every room, but this shit here is not about to happen!" I screamed.

"Fuck you!" she screamed back and left out the house.

Standing outside waiting on Eazy to pull up, I started growing impatient, so I walked slowly towards the direction he would be coming in. As I reached the next block, I saw his Charger coming around the corner. He pulled over and looked at me strangely as I sat down and closed the door. We pulled off and all I could think about was how I'm going to ask him about the money and when can I go home.

As soon as I got in the car, I turned his music off and folded up my arms.

"Yo ma, didn't they tell you to never touch a black man's radio?" he said and turned it back up and I turned it back down. "Yo lil mama what's good? Who are you trying to boss up on like this is yo shit? I don't know if you grew balls since you've been home, but this ain't that," he said, causing me to get more pissed.

I was already pissed at my dumb ass sister and now I'm pissed because he got me wasting my time when I could be trying to find me another job and handle my own shit so a bitch can never throw up in my face what the fuck they do or did for me.

"Eazy, my sisters said that you've been paying our rent every month, why didn't you tell me?" I asked.

"I didn't think I had to tell you. What I do is what I do. You are over at my brother's crib living the life of luxury and shit. I couldn't have them out on the streets. Just cause I don't fuck with you doesn't mean I can't keep them straight.

"If you're paying my rent then why am I even here with Blaise still. Don't get me wrong Blaise and I have become cool as fuck, but I have a life too."

"Oh, so you're trying to get back to your life of crime? Keep playing with people shit and somebody is gone come after your ass. You're lucky me having you look after my brother was all I had you to do. I'm from the streets and a nigga or a bitch stealing from me has never sat well. You're lucky yo ass is halfway cute or that face would've been fucked up by my lil' cousin and she's really bout that life. You don't have that much longer left then you can take your ass on."

He turned up the radio and did the dash to the store. I sat there in silence the entire way there. I didn't like how he blew up on me and I wanted to punch his ass in the mouth.

I decide to get out and grab me something to drink. I noticed this fine ass Morris Chestnut look alike just staring at me. Once he saw Eazy get back in the car, he started approaching me. I tried so hard not to look at him as he walked to me but this man was sexy as fuck. You could see his muscles through his shirt.

"Hello, I'm Jordan, nice to meet you," he said as he extended his arm out to me. "I'm Cherish, it's nice to meet you as well."

"I saw you with lil' man and I didn't know if that was your guy or anything, but I decided to step to you anyway."

"No, he's not my man, more like my big brother nothing more nothing less."

"That's good to hear, ma. Are you still working at Victoria Secret?"

"Wait, how did you know I worked there?" Ok, now I'm about to walk away from his ass cause he know a little more than he should and I'm started to feel real uncomfortable.

"I was in there one day with my ex and I noticed you then, but of course I was with my girl, so I couldn't approach you."

"Oh Ok, I thought you were on some stalker shit. I was about to call my brother out the car real quick." I laughed, but he didn't think it was funny.

"There's no need to call your lil' guard dog on me, we're good, ma. So can I have your number or what?"

"Sure, why not! It's 901-725."

"Aye, get cho ass in the car, yo ass is out here talking to a crackhead Wesley Snipes!" I heard Eazy yell from the car window. He seemed really bothered when he saw Jordan trying to talk to me.

"Damn, really Eazy?" I screamed out to him.

"Well, I guess I'll get it the next time Miss Cherish, but your lil' guard dog is calling out for you," he said as I turned to walk away.

"Yea, next time." I couldn't stop thinking about how Eazy just tried to make a scene with me.

"What was that all about?" I asked.

"What you mean, I was ready to go so I made your ass hurry the fuck up and stop questioning why I do and say shit, ma," he quipped, turning his radio up and speeding back to Blaise's house. He dropped me off in front of the house.

"Tell Blaise I'll be right back," Eazy said as I got out the truck.

Blaise always has his back door unlocked so I started walking around the back and as I passed the front window I saw these two men with masks on in the house with Blaise. One standing, holding a gun at him and the other one destroying the place. I'm guessing he's looking for drugs or maybe money. I remembered Eazy gave me his number a while back for emergencies. I sent a quick text to him so they wouldn't hear me talking.

Me: *It's Cherish. You need to get back to Blaise's house ASAP. Someone is in the house, HURRY!*

Lil' Bitch Nigga: *Aight here I come, shorty.*

I had to laugh at myself at what I stored his name under.

I peeked back in the window one last time before I went inside to help him my damn self. I can't wait on Eazy to get here Blaise would be dead by then.

I ducked down, went inside my purse and slowly made my way into the house. Easing down the hall, I peeked around the corner to see where the guys were standing.

"Where's the work and the money?" the dude asked Blaise.

"I don't have anything and who said it would be at my crib? You're wasting your fucking time, bruh!" Blaise spat back. He took his gun and knocked Blaise out and when I saw that, something clicked inside of me and I came from around the corner with my gun aiming right at dude's head.

Pow! Pow!

The other guy goes to draw his gun, but I was too quick for him.

Pow! Pow!

I ran over to Blaise and attempted to wake him, "Blaise come on, wake up, wake up," I said while smacking him in the face. I remembered hearing Eazy say something about they had more stuff here and he would be back so they can take it to the lake house. I started looking for everything, because I'm sure those nosey ass neighbors called the police when they heard the gunshots so I had to move quickly.

I went back over to Blaise and lifted him off the chair and started towards the door. As we made it outside, I saw Eazy pulling back in. As soon as he saw me dragging Blaise he ran out the truck. "What happened, what happened?" he asked frantically.

"When you dropped me off, it was two guys in the house trying to rob him. I snuck in and once I saw him hit Blaise with the gun, I just started shooting and I killed both of them; they wanted drugs and money. One guy knocked Blaise out when he said he had nothing and that's when I started shooting.

"Damn, the shit is still in the house!" he started running to the house,

"No! Eazy stop, I've got it!" I screamed out making him stop in his tracks.

"You got it?" he asked with a confused look on his face.

"Yes, just get him to your car and leave. I'll tell the police I was the only one here and they came in and tried to rape me, but I got away and I killed them. Now go and get Blaise to your crib and stay with him until he wakes up."

"Are you sure that's a smart move, Cherish?" Eazy asked.

"Yes, I'm sure! Now go."

I didn't tell him that I know the chief of police and he could make anything go away for me. He and my mom used to date before I was born and before she became an addict. He stops by every now and then to help out saying that he owes it to us to do whatever he can as a friend of our mom. A few moments later, I heard sirens coming up the street pulling me out of my thoughts. I ripped my shirt just a little and tugged on the neck of it to make it look like they were grabbing me and I started to make myself cry. I was the queen of making myself cry. I took drama in high school and they taught me how to pull emotions from everywhere to make a scene more believable.

I jumped up and ran to the officer. "Oh, thank you, thank you for coming!" I screamed.

"Calm down ma'am, I'm Officer Tucker; a neighbor called and said they heard gunshots."

"Yes, I was sleeping in my bed and two guys came in and tried to rape me. One was destroying my house and the other was trying to force himself on me!" I spat, forcing more tears out my eyes. "Where are they now?"

"They are in the house, I- I- I got away and one tried to pull a gun on me, but I sleep with a gun under my pillow for protection because I live alone so I keep it close. As he started to rush towards me, I shot him and then the other one came in the room and tried to attack me too, I just closed my eyes and started shooting again. I was scared and didn't know what to do, I didn't mean to kill them I just wanted them to leave." I started to cry harder, like real crocodile tears. He began to radio in the incident and called a medic to come.

"I'll be back, I have to go and check things out."

I saw Eazy coming back around the corner slowly. My heart dropped, I thought he would come back and say the wrong thing to the cops. He pulled into the driveway and got out. He ran over to me like this was his first time seeing me. The police came back outside and started walking towards us.

"Baby, are you ok? Why are the police here? Did something happen?" Eazy asked instantly putting the look of 'what the fuck' on my face.

"I'm sorry sir but you can't be here, this is a crime scene," Officer Tucker stated.

"Fuck that, this is my girl I'm not leaving her here. If anything, I'm getting her out of here. She just told me what happened so I'm sure she's afraid and I want to get her out of here!" Eazy spat. I pulled out more tears and collapsed in Eazy arms.

He smelled so good. He picked me up and cradled me like a baby in his big strong arms and all I could think about was how I wanted to make sweet love to him. But I knew all of this was just a front and wouldn't last long. More cops and the ambulance pulled up with a coroner not far behind. They loaded up the bodies, took my statement and after I told them my stepdad was the chief of police, they let me call him.

"He wants to speak to you," I said as I handed Officer Tucker his phone back, then next thing I saw was everybody loading up and leaving, no more questions were being asked. They even sent a cleanup crew over to clean the house up.

Chapter 10

Eazy

I had to go back and get her. I couldn't let her take the wrap for this shit, even though she sounds like she knew what she was doing, I had to be sure. After I took my brother to my crib around the corner, I made sure he was straight first then I left to check on Cherish. I pulled up and saw her sitting on the ground with no police in sight, I guess he was in the house. I have to think of something quick to explain why I'm here. I ran over to her and grabbed her up.

"Baby, are you ok? Why are the police here? Did something happen?" I saw the look on her face wanting to know why I called her baby, but I was hoping she would play along. The officer started to come outside. I had to throw this Uncle Tom ass nigga off some kind of way so I can get her out of here.

"I'm sorry sir but you can't be here, this is a crime scene," the officer stated.

"Fuck that, this is my girl I'm not leaving her here. If anything, I'm getting her out of here. She just told me what happened so I'm sure she's afraid, and I want to get out of here!" I spat.

"We have to get more information from her sir you can't take her anywhere right now." Cherish instantly started crying hard tears; it even had me thinking something was wrong with her.

This lil' bitch is acting her ass off, I said to myself then I felt her pass out in my arms. I instantly grabbed her up and walked her to the backseat of my car.

She smelled so good, the wind was blowing hard, so her hair was blowing across my face and all I smelled was fruits and berries. I felt her face turn into my chest and take a deep breath. I whispered in her ear "I still don't fuck with you," then she all of a sudden woke up and told the officer her dad was the chief of police and to call him. She never told me this shit or I would have never let her police ass in my brother spot. She probably sent the guys over here then things went left.

"Here, he wants to speak to you," she said to the officer. I'm not sure what she said, but he got rid of everyone quickly with no more questions asked. We got into my truck and started heading towards my house, where I left Blaise.

I turned the radio off so I could clear my head on all that just happened, and I did the dash to my crib. She got out the truck and I noticed how thick shorty had gotten. Once we got inside, she went to the couch to check on Blaise.

"Hey brother," she said as she kneeled down in front of him and rubbed his face where he had a bruise. "Are you ok?"

"Yea. I'm good, I heard you took care of those dudes for me. I saw you when you peeped through the window and ducked down, by then they had taken my blindfold off and still had their face covered. That's when I tried to get them to leave, I didn't want you to come in and get hurt. I didn't know you would be the one doing the hurting tho, sis. Where did you learn to shoot like that?"

"Well, once my mom left, it was just my sisters and I. I had to make sure we were protected at all times, so we started going to the gun range every weekend and having target practice at my stepdad's place."

When I heard her say stepdad that made me think of what she said earlier "Speaking of stepdad, so yours is the C.O.P., huh?" I asked.

"He's not really my stepdad, he's just a guy my mom dated before I was born and he has been around ever since. When she left he always came back to make sure we were good and made sure we had food to eat, and shit like that."

"So you didn't send those guys to my brother crib, right?" By the look she gave me, I already knew she didn't, but I had to hear her say it or she was about to end up like those dudes.

"Eazy. I'm not that girl! Now granted, I did steal from you and I regret it every day, but I would never send anyone out to do any harm to Blaise."

She stood up and lifted up her shirt and pulled a pair of Blaise big sweatpants down. My mouth dropped open after I saw what she did. Her body was looking pretty damn good might I add, but she was wrapped in my work. She had duck taped my shit around her thighs and stomach. No wonder shorty was looking so damn thick. I couldn't believe she went through that trouble to make sure we didn't get caught with anything and risked her life by putting it on her.

"I knew they wouldn't search me once I let them speak to my dad, but does this look like a person who set you up? Would I go out my way to make sure you still had all yo shit?" She questioned. I felt bad as hell, I was trying my hardest not to like this bitch. I hate a thief, but I love a loyal bitch.

"Yea well you may have won my brother over, but you have to do a helluva lot more than wrap your body in coke to convince me you won't steal from me again," I replied as I stood up and grabbed my shit off the table.

"Don't mind him, he will eventually come around. He just hates for people to steal from him. This kid stole his coloring box in first grade, he beat his ass and got suspended from school. So he's felt this way about a thief ever since then," I heard Blaise try to explain to her.

"I'm about to call up Rocko to see if he can come back down sooner, we have to get out of here. I'm sure those niggas had people knowing they were coming to your spot, so I'm almost certain more niggas will be coming."

This shit is about to get way out of hand. This is exactly why I always told Blaise's ass to never keep shit at the house, and stop allowing these random ass hoes in his spot. Both of them could have been dead, it was a good thing Cherish was there to save his ass.

"Rocko will be here in the morning," I stated as I went to sit next to my brother to make sure he was straight. I could see that

Cherish was a down ass bitch. Nobody would have ever done no shit like this for us.

"Say E," my brother said pulling me out of my trance. "I heard one of the nigga's voices before man, but I just couldn't put my finger on that shit. He knew too much about our shit that's the bad part!" he stated.

"I told your ass about having shit at the house, bitches in the house, and leaving that fucking door unlocked. It could've been worse. You better be lucky Cherish was there to save yo ass! Anyway, I'm about to lie down I'll catch y'all ass in the morning."

A few hours went by and I could hear them coming upstairs. Blaise had a room here and Cherish was going to the guest room.

***

The next morning

"Damn babe, that shit feel good, don't stop," I said as she continued to swallow my dick, she took my nine inches down her throat with ease, lil' mama didn't gag once.

"Does it feel good, baby?" She asked as she let out a sexy ass moan while playing with her pussy.

I could see how wet the pussy was from here, just by looking at her fingers sliding in and out with juices all over them. I couldn't wait to taste her. I didn't want to explode in her mouth because she was so much better than that. I lifted her up and laid her on the bed, spreading her legs as wide as they could go. I kissed her from her feet up to her inner thighs and began sucking gently on her clit. I knew she would taste sweet, the freshness of her pussy made me go dumb, as I flipped her over and ate her from the back. Shorty had ass for days. As I licked her pussy, I smacked her on her ass. I could tell she liked that shit cause every time I hit her, I could feel her pussy getting wetter and wetter. Her moans grew louder and louder. I could tell she was about to reach her peak. I stood up and put my dick inside that tight pussy. We both let out a moan and she gently started throwing that ass back on me. I pulled her up close to me so I could kiss on her neck. Grabbing her by the waist, I started pounding that pussy. She threw one leg around me and flipped herself over on her back then pulled me closer with her legs, wrapping both around me. I lifted her up and pinned her to the wall.

"Damn, ma. You gone have a nigga sprung. I'ma make sure this is my pussy for life." I shot my seed inside of her and I could feel her cumin' on my dick at the same time. I slowly let her down and she walked over to the shower in my bedroom and turned the water on. "Cherish, you gone be mine forever, I know I just got that ass pregnant."

Knock! Knock!

A knock at my bedroom door woke me up from this crazy ass dream I was having about Cherish. As soon as I opened the door there she stood with these big ass shorts on that Blaise must have found her in my other room, a wife beater, and no bra. Shorty could make anything look good as hell.

"What?" I spat, causing her to jump as I opened the door.

"Do you mind taking me to my house so I could grab some clothes? I have nothing here and everything I had was at Blaise's house; I don't want to go back there just yet," she asked as she came into my room and sat down on the Lay-Z-Boy.

"Yea, I'll be down there shortly."

I like to catch the news before I did anything. Memphis news was always stupid as hell; they didn't care what they did a story on as long as they were putting something out there. Turning to channel 5 news I saw two faces flash across the screen. I turned my volume up loud as hell so I could hear.

"Yo, Blaise come here!" I yelled out to my brother as he sat on the couch. He started coming up the stairs and into my room.

"Two men Al Pacino Carson, who goes by the name of Chino and another young man Lorenz Bishop were found shot and killed in a home off California Avenue. There are no leads to what exactly took place. Looks like it could have been a robbery gone bad. There are no suspect in custody at this moment."

"I knew I recognized that fucking voice, it was my best friend Chino. Why would he do something like this to me? I have given this man everything including the shirt off my back. If I ate, we ate, simple as that. That was my guy. How couldn't I tell he was a wolf in sheep clothes. Eazy, you always made sure we both were straight and this is how he repays us. As far as I'm concerned, this nigga got exactly what he deserved. My damn best friend, man! Shit like this makes me wanna kill his grandmother!" Blaise yelled.

"You're talking crazy now, bruh. We will discuss this shit later, I'm about to take shorty to her sister's house and then pick Rocko up from the airport!" I replied as I got up and grabbed my keys.

I can't do anything but shake my head at all this bullshit that was going on. It's amazing what can happen in a day, all over one careless mistake Blaise's dumb ass made now it's two dead niggas and more to come, but I'll be damned if I end up being one of them.

Chapter 11

CeCe

As we headed towards my place, I looked out the window and pretended to play on my phone so it wouldn't seem so awkward in here. I wonder what's on his mind. I can't believe his homeboy was one of the guys that came in the house.

"Cherish, I want to thank you for saving my brother. I don't know what I would have done without him. I know I said I didn't give a fuck about what you did, but I do. I've been being an asshole since day one, even though I had my reasons. Even after I made you work for me, you still kept it real and made sure he was straight and the police didn't take my shit. I was going to have you stay a little while longer, but you can go home and stay. I'm sure your sisters miss you and I shouldn't have kept you from them for so long. It took me to almost lose my brother to realize that family is very important. Just make sure yo ass don't go back to stealing people shit, especially mine, anyway," Eazy said jokingly.

"Thank you, I really do miss them and if there is anything you guys need, or if you need me to help you with anything let me know. Blaise is like a little brother to me so I know I will always stay in contact with him," I said as I looked over at him and smiled.

I started to feel the vibration from my cell phone. "Do you mind turning that down a little, my sister Karma is calling me?"

"What's up sis, I'm headed home right now. You must miss me?" I asked and all I could hear was screaming in the phone.

"CeCe, it's Cocoa. Karma has been shot!" My heart dropped and I instantly started to cry.

"What, how, why, where is she?" I couldn't get one question out without asking another one. So much was running through my head at that moment, so I began to pray for my sister. I didn't know how severe the injury was so I tried not to panic, but it didn't work. I was literally losing my damn mind.

"What's wrong, Cherish?" Eazy asked.

"It's my sister Karma, she's been shot. PLEASE HURRY UP SO I CAN GET THERE NOW!!" I screamed.

"Cocoa, please tell me she's ok. What happened?" I asked hysterically. As I heard sirens in the background, the phone hung up.

"Eazy, drive this fucking car I have to get to my sisters" I pleaded.

As we pulled up to the apartment all I saw was lights everywhere. I had just spoken to Karma this morning, I can't believe this shit. If it isn't one thing it's another.

As I start to run up the stairs, I saw them bringing her down on a stretcher. I dropped down to my knees and started to cry out to God. *"God, why did you let this happen to my sister? That's my best friend; I can't lose her, fix this Lord, please fix this!*

Karmaaaa... Karmaaaa... nooooo!" I started crying out for her to get up. I started running to the stretcher to unzip the body bag and I was caught by Eazy.

"Let me go now, put me down, I have to see her!" I screamed as I got loose from his arms.

I saw Cocoa at the top of the stairs crying while being held back by the police. A crowd started to gather around the caution tape. Eazy came and helped me up off the ground.

"This is all your fault, if I was home with her this would've never happened, she would still be alive, it's because of you, my sister is gone. You got me cooped up in the fucking house over bullshit, Eazy! I am supposed to protect my sisters; I can't believe I let her down like that. Who am I supposed to talk to now, huh? They didn't have to kill her, Eazy. Ugggggh!!! I can't believe this!" I screamed.

"Cherish, this is not my fault, you can't blame me for this. You and I both know why you have been at my brother's crib so don't try to flip this shit now," he said as he tried to reach out to me for comfort.

"Don't touch me!" I spat, as I ran upstairs to my sister. I grabbed her and she cried in my arms.

"I'm sorry CeCe, it's my fault she's gone; I shouldn't have had him here. I knew the rules and I wanted to be grown and run shit, I didn't listen and it cost my sister her life. She's gone and it's all my fault!" she continued to scream and cry. As the police walked down the stairs I asked her what happened.

"Dr. King popped up at the house this morning on some crazy shit, demanding that I have sex with him again and after we finished, he refused to pay. He started calling me a whore and saying how he will never pay for sex. Telling me either I was going to keep giving it to him willingly, or he will take it every time he wanted it. We started to fight over the money and Karma walked in to help me after she heard me screaming. She jumped on his back and started punching him in the head so he would let me go. The next thing I know, I heard a gun go off twice and she dropped to the floor. He shot her twice in the stomach, CeCe. I can't fucking believe this, how could I have been so stupid? He should've taken me instead, not my sister. She shouldn't have to pay for my sins."

I was trying to hold it together but I couldn't the tears started to flow. Eazy started walking up the stairs towards us.

"Cocoa, do you know who did this?" He asked.

"Yes, it was my therapist, Dr. King, but he ran off after he shot her."

"Aight, I've got you. I'll be back," he said as he turned and started going back down the stairs. I wasn't concerned about where he was headed; my mind was on my sister.

"Hello, I'm Officer Malik Perkins; I need you two to come down to the police station for some questions. You can get into the car with Officer Paris Petty."

"Ok, whatever we have to do to help, we will." After getting up off the ground, I glanced into the apartment and saw all of Karma's blood on the floor. I just dropped to my knees and began crying out to God again.

"Lord, what did she do to deserve this? Just give her back so I can tell her I love her and I'm sorry for not being here when she needed me."

"She wasn't supposed to die like this, Cocoa," I said.

"I know it's hard, but you will get through this. We will find the guy who did this and I personally will make sure he never see the light of day again," Officer Petty said as she helped me stand to my feet.

The car ride to the station seemed like it took forever. Cocoa was sitting next to me with Karma's blood all over her shirt. I began to cry at the sight of it. I couldn't believe she was gone, man... *fuck!* I thought to myself.

Arriving at the police station, they took us into interrogation room three. I was pissed at the fact they didn't let Cocoa change her clothes before heading up here. We waited in the room a little while before a detective came in.

"I'm Detective Long and I'm sure you've already met Officer Paris Petty. Now, Chloe Carter, you want to start by telling me how you know Dr. King and what he was doing at your place?" He asked, while placing a pen and notepad on the table.

She went into details on what happened and gave him the name and address of the guy. I couldn't help but notice how good the detective looked. He stood about 6'2, chocolate smooth skin, perfect teeth, and from what I could see through his button-up polo shirt, his body wasn't too bad either.

"Hey girls, I tried to get here as fast as I could when I heard the news." In walked, the chief of police my stepdad Chief Kevin Perkins. "Are you girls ok? I'm going to find out who did this and we will make sure he get the time he deserves!" he spat. "Chloe, are you ok?

"Yea, I'm fine I just wish they would've let me change clothes first," she replied, looking down at the bloody shirt she had on.

"I've got a clean t-shirt in my office; you can go and put it on."

"Ok, thanks!" she said as she got up and left out the room.

After sitting there almost an hour I decided to go and see where she was. I passed all of the officers and made my way to Chief Perkins office, but she wasn't there. Walking down the hall, I went into the ladies bathroom and all I could hear was the sounds of someone having sex. I wasn't sure if it was Chloe or not so I hurried out the bathroom and just stood by the door, hoping she would eventually walk past me. The sounds got louder and louder and I'm surprised no one was hearing anything.

"Damn, you taste so good," I heard the gentleman say with the sounds of moans following.

"Hmmm, shit daddy, I've missed you so much, fucccck!"

Now, I'm almost sure that's my sister's voice. She's so fucking disrespectful; our sister just got killed less than two hours ago and she in here getting her ass wet. I cannot fucking believe her.

This should have been a fucking wake-up call. It's because of the stupid ass men she fuck with that my sister is gone, and this is what the fuck she does. I need to walk away before I fucking spazz out on her ass in this police station, but I just had to see who she was in there with. The door opened up breaking me from my thoughts and out walked Chloe and Detective Long. I couldn't do anything but shake my head at her in disgust.

"Really, Cocoa?" I said as I turned and walked away. I had to leave because I felt her face was just anxious to be hit by my fist.

Chapter 12

Cocoa

I couldn't believe what happened; my sister is gone over $2,000 funky ass dollars. Dr. King and I have been messing around since my first visit to him, and he never had a problem with paying me before, so why now? I can't wait till they find his ass so I could ask him why he did it. My sister had so much going for herself. Since Cherish has been gone she enrolled in the University of Memphis and went on an interview for a couple jobs. She was going to tell CeCe when she came back to the house again. Now everything is all fucked up because of Dr. King's bitch ass. Better yet, I hope they find him before I do, or it's gone be hell. I will personally make sure his wife knows what type of person he is when I deliver this video of us fucking in her bed, and of course I'll make sure my face is blurred out.

The door came open to interrogation room three where Cherish and I were waiting, and it was a Detective Long. I've been sleeping with him since I was eighteen, so as soon as he came in my pussy instantly got wet. I could see the way my sister was eyeing him, but she can calm down because that's my meat right there. He's the only one I never made pay because he was so damn sexy and that tongue he had was pure gold. Yea, yea, I know my sister just died and I promise you I am really hurt behind it, but this dick will make me mourn her more easily. Detective Long had the longest dick I've ever seen. I knew he was from New Orleans the first time I had sex with him, those niggas down there be carrying that heavy weight between their legs, and the way he said my name with that accent made a bitch weak.

"Chloe Carter, so you want to tell me how you met Dr. King and why was he at your house?" Detective Long asked.

Damn it, I wasn't prepared for these questions, I can't let him know what I do and how I make my money. He has never met Cocoa the freak-a-leak, he's only met Chloe Carter the good sister, who was abandoned by her mom at a young age and was taken care of by her big sister, Cherish. I had to think fast.

"Dr. King is my therapist. I started seeing him a few months ago to help me move on past my mom leaving us. He came over to do a session at my house and after a while, he started looking at me mad funny, and it creeped me out. The next thing I know he was trying to get on top of me. I started screaming and crying and that's when Karma came in to help me, and he shot her." Tears started to fill my eyes, but I was trying my hardest to be strong.

"We are going to do everything we can to bring him in, in the meantime is there anything I can do for you both?" He looked over at CeCe and she had the sexiest seductive look on her face I've ever seen. "Please let me know," he said as he left out the room and shortly after my mom's ex came in and offered me a t-shirt.

I knew that would be a good reason for me to go and catch up with Detective Feel Good. I caught him just before he went into his office and lead him into the bathroom.

I wasn't expecting CeCe to be standing by the damn door when we came out, I know this is going to look soo bad. I really need to change man. I've been with so many men, and I can't even count without having to use someone else's hands too. I put my head down in shame when I saw the look on my sister's face. She turned and walked away and I followed slowly behind her. I never even got a chance to change my damn shirt.

"Ok, are you headed to get us now?" I heard her ask someone on the phone.

As we stood outside in silence, a few moments later a big truck pulled up and Eazy and Rocko were inside. "Hi," I said as I slid into the truck.

"What's up, shorty," Rocko replied as he looked down at all the blood on my shirt. "Here man." I looked up and he was taking his black polo t-shirt off and handing it to me. "I know you don't want to ride around with that shirt on, ma." I tried to give a smile to him.

"Thanks," I said softly and took off the bloody shirt and threw it out the window. Looking out of the window, I started to reflect on all of the good times I had with my sister, and then all of the times we argued, all I could do was cry! CeCe moved closer to me and held me tight.

"Say ma, stop all that damn crying and look on the floor behind you," Eazy requested.

My sister and I both turned around immediately and there he was, Dr. King tied up and blindfolded.

"Oh my god!" CeCe yelled out.

"Come on ma, I know you ain't scared of a dead body, well about to be dead body. You laid two to rest yo damn self!" Eazy reminded Cherish.

"I'm not scared, I just wasn't expecting him to be in the car. What are you going to do with him?"

"You mean what are you going to do with him?, I'm not doing anything, I did my part by finding him, with the help of Rock, of course, the rest is up to y'all."

We rode about forty-five minutes longer and ended up at Eazy's lake house. They pulled him out the back and into a storage house, where he kept a small boat. We followed them inside and closed the door. I snatched his face cover off, so he could see exactly who was about to fuck his world up.

I gave him a two piece to the face to wake him up, his eyes grew larger as he focused in on my face.

"Chloe... Chloe, baby I'm so sorry, I didn't mean to shoot her. It was an accident, please let me go. I'm sorry, please. I hope she's ok!" he cried out. It felt like all of his words were going into one ear and out the other one.

I wasn't trying to hear that bullshit he was spitting. All I wanted at that moment was my sister back and if I couldn't have her because of him, then this cracker ass had to die too. Cherish sat down and watched me beat the shit out of him, with her feet splashing the water back and forth. I guess she felt like he was my problem so I had to get rid of him. Usually, I wouldn't fight, but today I must have had my sisters strength, cause I was giving his ass the business.

Rocko handed me a gun. "You know you fucked up right? You killed my sister," I said, as I took a butterfly knife out my purse, jammed it into his thigh, and twisted it. He let out a loud cry.

"Just kill me already!" he screamed with tears filling up in his eyes.

"Fuck no, you didn't think I was going to just shoot you in the head, nooooo that's letting you take the easy way out. My sister didn't die instantly, she laid there and suffered until the ambulance came and removed her body. The only difference between you and her is we won't need an ambulance for you. I'm going to shoot you twice in the stomach, just like you did Karma. I'm going to watch you gasp for air and cry out for help, just like I had to do with Karma. Then I'm going to kick yo bitch ass into this lake. But first..." I kneeled down in front of him, unzipped his pants, and pulled his dick out. "...it's a shame all of this had to go to waste."

Shhhhhk! Shhhhhhk! was the sound the knife made as it tore through the shaft of his dick.

"Remind me to never fuck over this bitch right here!" Rocko yelled out, followed with Eazy laughing.

Pow! Pow!

I could hear the bullets tearing through his stomach and that instantly made my heart smile. Eazy tied some weights around his ankles and kicked his ass into the lake. I felt a relief after I saw the splash of water come up from his body falling in. Sitting down next to CeCe, I looked at her eyes holding back tears. Even though he was dead, it still didn't change the fact that our sister isn't here anymore.

"Let's go inside," Eazy requested.

"This has been a very interesting two days, yesterday it was Cherish popping two people and now today it's Chloe. It doesn't look like either of you have the heart to do something so cold, but I guess when you are put in a situation like this, it's either you or them. I know you guys don't want to stay at your apartment so you are more than welcome to crash at my house," Eazy said while taking a sip of his Hennessy.

"Sure, thanks. I really would appreciate that," CeCe said. *She was looking at Eazy the same damn way she looked at Detective 'Long Dick', I mean Detective Long,* I thought to myself.

"So have y'all fucked yet?" I asked, causing CeCe to damn near jump out her skin.

"Cocoa, no! Don't ask questions like that!" she stated as she turned red in the face, "You got angry, so either you have or you want to, sooo which one is it?"

"Can I have something to drink?" CeCe asked, trying to avoid my question. "Sure, I have Hennessy, and I have Vanilla Crown," Eazy replied.

"Damn, that's it, not even a bottle of water?"

"I'm hardly here so I only bring the necessities."

"And water isn't a necessity, Eazy?" She asked with a smirk on her face. I can definitely tell they will end up fucking sooner or later if they haven't already. We began taking shot after shot hoping to ease the pain until CeCe started to get sleepy.

"I guess I'll go ahead and head to bed, tomorrow we will decide on what we need to do about our place," Cherish said as she headed up the stairs. Eazy watched her as she got off the couch until he couldn't see her anymore.

"What's up with you and my sister, I know she ain't been gone for months just to work for you. What's really good?"

"Shit, I wasn't fucking with her but she kind of won me over when she helped my brother out of a jam yesterday. I was just telling her that she could go home for good, when you called her phone with that news about Karma."

"Speaking of yesterday," Rocko interrupted. "Did shorty really have her body wrapped in work and the cops didn't notice that shit?"

"Yea, man she did. That damn police that showed up you can tell he was fresh out of training. Once she called her mom's ex-boyfriend, shiidd that nigga made everybody leave, no questions asked!" Eazy with a little excitement in his voice

"We need to keep shorty on the team then, if she's that damn loyal!" Rocko stated. "She's gone be our lil' hitta, we already see Cocoa's bout that life too. Y'all mama raised y'all right," Eazy said.

"Nah my mama ain't raise us at all, my sister raised us. Our mama is a crackhead, she's on the streets or either dead. We haven't seen her in almost four years."

"Damn, shorty, my bad," Eazy replied.

"You're good, it's not a sensitive subject. It is what it is. CeCe did what she could to make sure we had everything we needed. She found a lil' hustle and that shit worked for her. Well, that was until she hustled you," I said as I looked over there to him.

"Oh, by the way, I have something for you." I went into my purse and pulled out five stacks. "This is what she owes you, right?" I asked, passing him the money.

"Really? Nah, shorty, you don't have to do that. Y'all need that bread now to help find a new spot, and where did you get all that from anyway?" He asked. I saw Rocko just sit back to listen since he already knew the deal.

"It's just money I had saved up. CeCe would never take my money so I always kept it for her just in case she needed it."

I couldn't tell Eazy I was really selling my pussy like it was giraffe pussy, sky high! I was always told you had to pay to play and

I lived by that. I kept my money in a safe place, I called it my hoe-01K plan.

"Also I wanted to tell you that I did know about the guys that tried to rob you. I used to talk to the guy Lorenz and I overheard a conversation with him and his cousin. I didn't think he would go through with it because the other guy said something about your brother being his best friend. He kept going on and on about how he work for you and you don't break bread with him, how you do your brother and he wanted to take everything from you. I should have said something to my sister, I really am sorry."

"It's cool, he got what he deserved then. You sister put that hot lead in his ass," Eazy replied with a smirk on his face.

Chapter 13

Ce-Ce

Walking into this place it all seemed so surreal. Never have I imagined that I would lose my sister in this way. By the time we came back home, everything was cleaned up, I guess Chief Perkins sent someone over to clean up for us. Heading into Karma's room I could no longer hold back the tears. Having flashbacks of us being up all night laughing and drinking my favorite wine "Sweet Walter" even though she didn't like it, she most definitely drunk it cause she didn't have to pay for it.

I sat on her bed surrounded by all of her old cheerleading trophies from competitions they won, and all of her honor roll certificates. She was twenty-two and she still had all this shit posted up just how she had it in the old house with mama. Knowing that I would never see her again made the tears flow like the Mississippi river. I held her pillow tightly wishing it was her. I couldn't believe Cocoa let something like this happen. Why couldn't she just listen to me and do like I said? No men in the house...No men in the house, that's the only rule I gave her and she couldn't even follow that. If she would have taken that shit somewhere else then Karma would still be here.

"You ok, ma?" Eazy asked as he walked into the room, interrupting me from my thoughts. He brought me here to get more clothes; I can't stay in this place anymore so we will stay with him until I find another spot.

"Yea, I'm cool. I'm just missing my sister."

"I know it will be a while before you can fully move past this. You and Cocoa are more than welcomed to stay as long as you like." He has been really good to me lately. We met in a horrible way but once we got past that, things got a whole lot better.

"We really do appreciate all of your help."

I smiled at him and leaned over to give him a thank you kiss on the cheek. That led to him kissing me on the lips. His tongue tasted so good, like he just popped a mint flavored Tic Tac in his mouth or some shit. His hand started going up my shirt, he kissed me with so much aggression as he played with my nipples. I pulled my shirt off and he unsnapped my bra and let my 38DD breasts hang. Lifting up one breast into his mouth, he sucked it and damn near made me cum. I haven't had sex in almost a year, so any little thing will have me nutting up. Slipping two fingers into my pussy, he massaged my clit so gently. "Hmmm, fuck, Eazy."

"You like that?"

"Yaasss daddy, I dooo…" I moaned out damn near creaming on myself.

He took his fingers and put it into his mouth. *I'm glad I had taken a shower before I left the house,* I thought to myself as I laid back on the bed waiting for him to put that big ass dick inside me. Instead, he greeted my pussy with several warm kisses, before he licked me from here to kingdom come. I lost track on how many times I came once I got to five. His tongue was like magic and it definitely had a bitch in love. After I came one last time he came up and gave me a kiss.

"I just wanted to make you feel good and take your mind off everything that has happened." He smiled at me, as I leaned up and wiped my juices from around his mouth.

"You did a damn good job, it completely took my mind off of everything. I wanted dick too, though, I'm sure that would've really helped me."

"Oh, you're gone get dick too, but when we are at my place, I don't want to make you squirt all in your sister's bed."

I turned around and noticed I was still lying on Karmas bed. "Oh shit!" I screamed as I jumped out of her bed.

"I can't believe I just did that, it was so disrespectful of me." I started to cry again thinking of my sister.

"Cherish calm down, it's my fault I shouldn't have taken it there with you. Go ahead and grab some clothes so we can go, ma," he said as he left out the room.

"I'm so sorry, Karma. I shouldn't have done that. Not even forty-eight hours after your death and here I am damn near about to fuck on your bed. I'm sorry sis, please forgive me," I said aloud as if I was talking directly to her. Looking back at her room one last time I turned the light off and walked away.

"Oh shit, I almost forgot to get the rest of Cocoa money out the room" her hoe-01K as she calls it, that girl needs serious help.

As we start to head to Eazy house, he did the dash the entire way there. I had to break the silence in the car, it was starting to get really awkward.

"So where did all that come from?" I asked in a shy tone.

"All of what?"

"Don't play," I said as I let out a little laugh. "You know what I'm talking about, boy." I looked over at him.

"You had my entire coochie in your mouth and now you want to act like you don't know what's going on."

"Ha ha ha you're real funny; yea, I did have that sweet pussy in my mouth. I mean, yea even though you fucked me when I first met you, it's hard to keep denying my attraction for you. You're bad as hell for real, ma! And I would love to get to know you more."

"What about all those lil' hoes you was buying shit for."

"Oh, you talking about the day you stole my bread."

"Stop it." I laughed out loud. "Yea, that day."

"Oh, those were for few of my brother and cousin bitches, not mine."

"Yea, I hear you! We will see, but yea I'm all for getting to know you, I mean hell my pussy was in your mouth already, so if you ask me that mean we go together." We both cracked up laughing together. As we waited at the light, I turned to look at him and saw someone with a mask running towards us with what I could see a gun behind his back.

"Eaaazzzzy, duck!" I screamed out as I pulled my gun out of my purse and started shooting as Eazy sped off.

"Fuuucccck! What the fuck man, what the fuck was that shit?" He questioned, looking around. I couldn't even reply at that moment my heart was beating out of my chest and all I wanted to do was get the fuck out of there.

"It probably was someone that knew those guys that came in on Blaise," I finally replied while still taking deep breaths.

"I knew they would come and try to retaliate, I didn't think it would be like that, though, I'm sorry for putting you in that situation," he stated.

"Don't worry about it, I'm just glad I was here with you. This shit is only going to get worse cause um..." I paused to look in the rearview mirror, "I'm pretty sure he's dead too." I let out a little laugh. We pulled into the house to tell Rocko and Cocoa what happened.

"Say bruh, where are y'all at?" Eazy yelled out for Blaise and Rocko.

"We're out back." They had a barbecue going while our ass was about to get shot up.

"Those fuck boys came at me with Cherish in the car. I didn't like that shit at all man. We were right there on Germantown Parkway and Farmington Boulevard. That lil' nigga came out of nowhere, they had to be watching us a minute to have someone at the fucking light waiting on us."

"You already know how we get down cuz, let's call our people and see if we can find out who this cat is and who we need to handle!" Rocko spat.

"I know where one of the guys that got killed stays, he used to fuck with my sister and I had to pick her ass up one night. His name is Lorenz and from what the news said his last name is Bishop. When I saw his name and picture come across the screen I actually already started asking people who he usually hangs with and where. Oh, and I can definitely give you his girl's location too. They supposed to get back to me by today. This is a very reliable source, so I'm sure he will have everything you need."

"That's what's up, make sure you get us that ASAP. Are y'all straight tho?" Blaise asked.

"Yea, we're good. Shorty took care of his ass too, she a true killer for real. I didn't even see him coming she yelled out duck, and you know with black folks when you say duck or run we do that shit and ask questions later! " he spat, making them laugh.

"Where's my sister?"

"She's upstairs waiting on you to bring the clothes," Blaise replied.

"Oh damn, I almost forgot all about those, let me go upstairs and give her these so she can wash that big ass of hers." I headed upstairs to the guest bedroom only to find my sister in a corner praying.

Father God,

I come to you as humble as I know how. I don't know where to start or if you are listening but I've always been told you hear a sinner's prayer. Lord, I have sinned like no other. I have gotten myself and those around me in some terrible trouble. I have fallen short and I need you to have mercy on my soul. Forgive me Lord for the lives I have messed up and for the bonds that I have ruined. I don't know what would make me turn to men when I could have turned to you. I should have believed that you would supply all my needs. Now, my sister is gone and I don't know how to make it without her. Lord, please, please forgive me. Cleanse me from the innermost part to the outermost part. Wash me white as snow, Lord make me whole again. I have lost all hope, I feel unworthy, I feel like all hope is gone, Lord, please have mercy, Lord, please forgive me. Father, I repent knowing that you can make me new. Lord if my words aren't enough please hear my tears. In Jesus name, I pray, Amen.

I walked over to her and gave her the biggest hug ever. This is the Cocoa I've missed. My sweet little sister, if God didn't feel the sincerity in that prayer, I know I did.

"That was beautiful sis. Everything is going to work out for us, I can promise you that. We are all we've got, so just know I have your back and you had better have mine. Just trust me is all I ask, I don't want you to go back to that old hoe you used to know." We bust out laughing together. *"God, I want you to keep both of us safe and secure, and if I have to kill someone again just forgive me in advance, Amen,"* I said.

"That part," Cocoa yelled out followed with a laugh. "So you're bout that life?" She asked jokingly.

"You already know, they better get down or lay down." I laughed, repeating a line off *State Property*. I love seeing my sister smile and laugh again. I was so attached to Karma, I pushed Cocoa away and as her big sister, I should have protected her too.

"Wash your ass and come downstairs, Rocko is about to put some meat on the grill and I ain't talking bout your mouth. I see the way you be looking at him." I laughed as I closed the door behind me.

Chapter 13

Eazy

"You should have asked about me before you sent those bitch made as niggas into my brother's crib. Apparently, you niggas didn't think this shit all the way through. I've got real hittas on my team!" I spat, before I hit his ass in the face with an iron bat.

"Some lil' bitch ran up on me a few days ago and my girl took care of his ass just like we're about to take care of y'all."

"We didn't have anything to do with that shit, Chino and Lorenz set this up!" one of the guys yelled out.

"Well, we already know what happened to Chino right? That nigga got fucked by my bitch too, right now she 3-0 and I'm trying to catch up with her. From the looks of the niggas in the room, we're about to be even."

"Mmmmm... mmmm... mmmm..."

"Nigga, don't you know it's tape over your mouth? Can't nobody understand that shit bitch. You niggas really are stupid!" I blurted, snatching the tape off his mouth and as soon as I did that nigga spit in my face.

Pow! Pow!

"See, he made the wrong move, and to think I was gonna kill him last. How does it go, those who are last will one day be first, or some shit like that and today was his lucky day," I spoke, wiping the spit off me.

"Say bruh, check these niggas pockets."

Blaise started going through their pockets pulling out money and drugs. "Leave the drugs, take the money, and you can keep that." I know it was at least ten stacks between the three of them but that's my baby brother so he can have that shit.

"Pick a number between 1 and 2?" Blaise asked the last two guys. This nigga was always playing games and shit. I didn't say anything. I just sat back and watched.

"1," the guy in a red polo shirt said.

"2," the one with no shirt said.

"Good, now y'all just made this shit easier for my brother. E, kill 2 first then number 1." And with no hesitation, I did just that.

Pow! Pow! Pow!

Mr. Red shirt got hit twice in the chest, I didn't mean to fuck his new polo up, seeing that this nigga still had the tags on. Mr. No shirt got hit once in the head. And that's only because that nigga's line was cut better than mine.

"Let's roll," Rocko said, standing up and heading to the door. "You didn't need me or Wale for this shit. I could've been chilling with my pretty young thang."

"You're right but things could have gone wrong, so it's good to have the extra hands bruh, so calm down. I'm about to get you to Chloe ass."

I turned the music up and did the dash to Wale crib and dropped him off. My brother, Rocko, and I went back to my crib. I was glad Cherish's lil' informant came through for us. I couldn't have those niggas coming to my house and fucking shit up.

Pulling into my driveway I noticed all of the lights were off. It's 7:30 so I know the girls aren't sleeping.

"Something ain't right," I said, checking my surroundings.

"What you mean, cuz?"

"You know I have sensors around my house so the lights pop on if anything moves. This big ass truck of mine pulled in and nothing happened like they were cut off. Get y'all guns out. Blaise, you go in through the upstairs window, it's a ladder on the side of the house. Rocko, you go in through the back, and I'll take the front."

Creeping up the steps I saw my curtains moving like someone was watching. "You might want to come out now if you know what's good for you!" I yelled.

Before I even got inside, I saw the lights pop on and shots going off. I opened the front door and saw two niggas laid out on my floor, and the girls tied up in a corner. Blaise and Rocko had already taken care of them.

One of the guys was old crackhead ass Wesley Snipes Cherish was talking to the other day.

"What the fuck, Cherish? I know you didn't invite him to my house!" I yelled.

"Hell no, Eazy. I thought it was one of y'all. They had the peephole covered and it was completely dark so I just assumed I couldn't see cause it was dark outside. When I opened it a little they ran in."

"Did he say anything to you?"

"Yea, he said he wanted all of the money I stole from him when he came in Victoria Secret with his girl."

"I thought you said that shit couldn't be traced back to you?"

"See after all these years nothing has been traced to me. When he approached me at the store I was wondering how he already knew where I worked," Cherish replied.

"Man, Ce you should've told me that shit then and I would've checked his ass. Pack some clothes I'm about to send a cleanup crew here, we going to Rocko's house. I still couldn't figure out how he even knew where I lived and about that dumb shit Cherish be pulling. If his ass found her and knows about that shit she pulled, then I'm sure everyone can easily find out. Seeing her in the corner tied up looking helpless, made me want to protect her ass every day. I've had a few bitches before, but over these past few months, I slowly stopped fucking with them. Don't ask why cause hell, I don't even know. Right now all I know is I had to keep shorty close.

***

Stepping into Rocko crib the smell of Kush and pizza hit my nose instantly. He went back to his crib when the girls started getting some clothes.

"Bruh, what you got going on?" I asked as I walked into the kitchen

"Shit, a nigga was hungry so I ordered up a few pizzas. I felt like kicking back and rolling up a fat ass blunt." A few moments later the girls walked into the kitchen and came around to sit on the bar stools next to me.

"CeCe, when you started smoking?" Cocoa asked and Blaise ass started laughing, I knew his ass had something to do with it then.

"See what had happened was," she said causing Blaise to laugh even harder.

"Blaise's crazy ass offered me a blunt one day and I've been hooked ever since."

I gave Blaise the side eye because I wasn't feeling that bullshit at all. CeCe leaned over to me and whispered in my ear pulling me out of my thoughts of beating my brother ass.

"Let's go outside," she stood up and grabbed my hand and lead me out the patio doors.

"I'll holla at y'all ass a little later," I said as we closed the door behind us.

It was dark as hell outside now, so I wasn't sure what she wanted to talk about. I sat down in one of the pool chairs and watched as she stripped down to her lace boy shorts and bra, then jumped into the pool. It was a nice night in August, Rocko pool was heated anyway so she was good. I watched as she swam back and forth then came out of the water to the edge of the pool where I was now sitting. She looked so fucking good with the water dripping off her body. Her hair instantly curled up in tight curls as the water touched it. She climbed out of the pool and walked over to me and lead me to a chair. I couldn't help but watch her ass sway from side to side. My dick was getting hard as a rock. She pulled my dick out and gave me the sloppiest head I've ever had.

"You said I could get dick later, well its later!" She said as she slipped her panties off, turned around backwards and eased down slowly on my dick. She didn't even give me a chance to respond. I wanted to let her know, I had AIDS and we had to use a condom.

Nah, I'm just fucking with y'all, a nigga's dick is clean, and her pussy is safe with me. For real I wanted to tell her ass to let's go to a bed, but hell outside is good too. I laid my head back, put my hands around her waist, and watched her as she handled my dick like a pro. I said I didn't like lil' mama smoking but if it made her like this, I need this bitch high every night.

"Hmmm, shit," she moaned out as she slowly bounced on my dick.

Her pussy was so damn good I had to think about church, to stop myself from nutting. Okay, wrong metaphor, I had to think about raindrops and drop tops or I was gonna bust all in her ass. I didn't take her as a freak by her demeanor, but I'm glad she kept this side of her a secret or Blaise as would've tried shorty a long time ago.

"I'm cumming baby, hmmm, cum with me," she purred. My dick must have had a mind of its own because as soon as she said that I exploded in her. She leaned her body back on mine and just sat there. Then I heard her ass snoring.

"What the fuck?" I said, followed by a laugh.

She was knocked the fuck out for real. I slid her all the way up off my dick and sat her down in the chair. I grabbed her panties, her clothes and put them back on her. I couldn't carry her back in the house like that. I cradled her in my arms, kissed her forehead and walked her back inside.

"Which room you want me to lay her in?" I asked while walking through the kitchen.

"Damn, you fucked her ass to sleep, huh?" Cocoa yelled out while looking down at my pants, causing me to look down.

I started laughing as I saw I forgot to put my own pants back on. Here I am standing with her in my arms knocked out fully clothed, and I've got on a polo t-shirt and an orange pair of polo briefs. I couldn't do nothing but laugh and shake my head as I headed into the room to lay her down.

Chapter 14

Cocoa

Rocko has been gone a month now and I can't get his fine ass off my mind for shit. When he was here we got a chance to kick it and talk a little bit. I swear it felt like I was back in high school. We talked about a lot, we laughed into the wee hours of the night, and when I woke up we were both lying on the couch and I was snuggled up in his big ass arms. For the first time a man actually gave me intimacy instead of just dick and for the first time, I was ok with that. Ever since then if he wasn't with Eazy and Blaise handling business, he was with me, taking me on dates and shit. I've never had a real date before, so everything was new to me. I figured after dinner that we would go to his house so I could repay him but apparently, that's not how things actually work. So when we pulled back up to Eazy house, he got out and came over to my side and opened the door.

"I didn't know a thug like you knew that he was supposed to open doors," I said jokingly.

"Well, that's why we are still getting to know each other, cause I see it's still a lot you don't know about me. Regardless of what I look like, on the outside, my mama raised a man."

"I hear you, so are you coming in?"

"Nah ma, I'm going back to my place."

"No night cap?"

"Ha, nah! No night cap just yet but I have something planned for tomorrow so be up and dressed by ten. No need to get fancy just wear something simple."

"Ok cool, just let me know when you are on the way."

I leaned up to give him a kiss and he turned away, my heart dropped into my stomach, I've never been rejected before. After he turned away I took a step back to look at him. He didn't even try to give me an explanation.

"I'll see you in the morning ma," he stated as he turned and got back in his truck and left me standing there taking deep breaths in my hand trying to see if my breath was funky or some shit.

I walked into the house only to see my sister and Eazy on the couch fucking each other's brains out.

"Don't run from me, take this dick, girl."

"Oooohhhh I'm cuminnn'... I'm cumminnn' ... I'm cumminnnn'!" she screamed out.

Well, I'm glad somebody was getting some cause I sure in the hell wasn't. I know sex should be the last thing on my mind but a bitch ain't had none in months. That's torture to a bitch that's used to fucking multiple times a day.

"Oh well, good thing the guest bathroom has a detachable shower head," I said aloud to myself as I walked upstairs. I love how Eazy had this room decorated, in black and gold. It was a king size bed in each room and my ass about to snuggle up with nobody.

After running my hot bath water, I heard my phone ding. A text from Rocko was on the screen. I shouldn't even reply to his ass. The nigga straight dodged my kiss like I'm nasty. That shit slick hurt my damn feelings.

My Future Zaddy: Thinking about you.

Me: I bet.

My Future Zaddy: What is that supposed to mean? What's wrong with you?

Me: Nothing, don't worry about it.

My Future Zaddy: Look ma, don't get shit twisted, just cause a nigga is nice to you and shit doesn't mean I'm a weak man. If I ask you what the fuck is wrong then yo ass need to tell me what the fuck is wrong. I don't like that nothing shit when you really have an issue.

Me: Why didn't you kiss me?

My Future Zaddy: Is that why you got an attitude cause a nigga didn't kiss you? Get the fuck out of here man for real. Look I'm about to go to bed have yo ass ready in the morning. Good night.

Me: Good night.

Whatever, I don't even have time for this bullshit. I turned my R. Kelly station on Pandora and zoned out to "12 play".

The warmth of the water relaxed my body. I laid back and turned the water on full blast, grabbed the shower head, lifted one leg out the tub, and practically made love to the shower head. I hope they couldn't hear me downstairs cause the nuts felt good and I'm not into holding back my moans, I don't care who's around.

Grabbing a big fluffy towel to dry my body off with, I continued letting my R Kelly station on Pandora play. I grabbed my cocoa butter and rubbed my body down. Yea, I know that lotion smelled like a black and mild but it made my skin so extra pretty and shit. I laid across the bed asshole naked until I drifted off to sleep.

***

Peep, peep, peep, peep,

My alarm started going off. I set it for nine a.m. so I could be ready when Rocko arrived. I rolled over to snuggle back under the covers a little while longer, but my body was stopped by something in the bed. I turned all the way over and it was Rocko.

"What the hell, Rocko? What are you doing here?" He was lying there with nothing on but his boxers snoring like a big ass bear, how could something look so good, make such an awful noise. "Rocko!" I called out, rocking him back and forth so he could wake up. "

What's up ma, lay back down it's not time to get up yet," he spoke in a raspy voice.

"What made you come over here?"

"I missed yo little slim thick ass, so I used my key to let myself in. Is it a problem?"

"No, it's not."

"Well, lay yo ass down." He pulled me back into his arms and we fell back to sleep for another forty-five minutes.

***

Walking out to his black Challenger, he grabbed my hand and opened the passenger door for me.

"So, where are we going?" I asked.

"Nothing major, ma, just sit back and ride."

Well, I'm glad I threw on something comfortable. I put on my black Adidas leggings with a black and white Adidas tank with my shell toe black Adidas. And I threw my hair into a high bun with my big gold hoop earrings.

After riding about twenty more minutes we finally stopped.

"Why are we here?" I asked with confusion in my voice.

"Look Shorty, you told me all about your past and I can't lie like it hasn't been replaying in my head. I just want the best for both of us."

"So you bring me to the health department, for what? To get tested?" I spat in a tone I didn't even recognize myself.

"Hell yea, I'm feeling the shit out of you and because of your track record, this is only right. I hope this doesn't make you feel uncomfortable. But this is why I didn't kiss you last night or why we haven't had sex yet. We're getting tested together. Now, are you coming or not?"

I can't believe this bullshit, who does stuff like this? He really brought me to a clinic. I always get tested every six months anyway, but the fact that he decided to surprise me with a trip to the clinic does make me feel some type of way.

"Yea, I'll go! But on one condition."

"What's that?"

"After they tell you my ass is clean, I want to feel my pussy all in ya mouth." I laughed, but I was dead ass serious.

"Aight shorty, I've got you."

I reached for the door handle only to get jerked back.

"I don't know who you're used to fucking with but no woman of mine will ever touch a door handle."

We got out the car and headed inside. We waited for thirty minutes before they called us to the back. Usually, you have to wait to get your test results back, but I take it Rocko knew someone that worked here, cause we got that shit back in twenty minutes. They read our results to us and then left out the room.

"Soooo do you want my pussy in ya mouth now or later? Or both?" I spat, letting out a little laugh.

"I would say now, but she just did a pap on you too and I'm sure you still got a lil' gel down there," he replied.

"You're so fucking stupid. Well, I guess that means later then, huh? Let's go so I can wash my ass, cause I really do still have some gel on my shit." We laughed as we left out the building.

I guess my prayer worked the other day, cause God has really been working on me these past few days. A few men called my cell phone wanting to see me and of course, spend some money and I deleted the message and kept watching this new movie called *Hidden Figures* with my sister. This quality time I've spent with her has been nothing short of amazing. If only Karma was here then this would really be one happy family.

Oh, I almost forgot, the next day after I cut off Dr. King dick, I did just what I told him I would do. I dropped the tape off to his wife with his dick in the box, it was unfortunate that his daughter answered the door, though, she might not want to open that gift box.

"What's going on with you and Rocko? I see you two are getting real damn cozy?" She asked, snapping me or of my thoughts.

"What's going on with you and Eazy? I saw y'all humping like rabbits on the couch last night."

"Bitch, don't answer a question with a question," she said, making me laugh hysterically.

"Girl, whatever! Nothing is up with us, this nigga took me to the clinic today."

"For what? Are you pregnant already?"

Giving her the side eye, I replied, "I know you lost your damn mind. He took me to get tested; he knew more about me than I thought his ass did."

"You're straight, though, right?" She asked with hesitation in her voice like she was almost scared of the response.

"Yes, Cherish Patrice Carter, I'm clean! But I told him that, though, and I also said once they tell you that I am clean you have to put my pussy all in your mouth," she burst out laughing.

"Bitch, you did not tell him that?" She quizzed.

"Now, you know me. I won't bite my tongue for no one. If he was bold enough to take me to the clinic, then I was bold enough to ask him to eat my booty like groceries." She tossed a pillow at my head.

"Ok, that's enough I'm going to bed cause you have officially lost it. Good night, sis."

"Good night sissy."

Chapter 15

Rocko

Me: Make sure you are ready by six p.m. I have something planned for us.

Miss Fat Ass: It better not be another trip to the clinic or we gone fight, lol.

Me: Nah shorty, we're good now. Just be dressed and this time I want you to be uncomfortable.

Miss Fat Ass: Uncomfortable?

Me: Yea, if what you had on yesterday was comfortable, I need you to be uncomfortable in something sexy and tight as hell, just don't look like a thot walking outside or you will be sent back in the house.

Miss Fat Ass: Lol you're really funny, mister. I'll see what I can do. See you later, I'm about to go to breakfast with Cherish.

I had to send a quick text to lil' mama, I've been watching people get killed these last few days so now I need her to help me unwind and take my mind off all this shit. On top of me letting her know once I leave this time I'm not coming back, and I want her to come back with me.

Ding! Ding!

A text came through pulling me from my thoughts.

Crazy Bitch Dorian: *I miss you and I really want you back. I gave you your space to clear your head, now it's time to come back home.*

Me: *Come back home? I know yo ass ain't back in my condo.*

Crazy Bitch Dorian: *This is our condo nigga, you can't just quit me. I've been here for a few weeks now waiting for you to come back. I'm starting to get real impatient with your ass.*

I know she must have lost all her mind, talking to me like she runs shit. She just don't know I will send my pit bull over there on her and y'all already know Chloe is definitely with the shit.

Me: *Dorian I'll give you to 6:30 to get out my shit or else!*

Crazy Bitch Dorian: *Or else, what? Are you gone choke me again?*

Me: *You just better make sure you are gone.*

I need to get my ass back to New York before I kill this bitch, I thought to myself.

***

Pulling up at Applebee's to meet Eazy and Blaise at the bar, I got out quickly cause a nigga was hungry as hell.

"What's up cuz? I'm glad lil' mama finally let you out the pussy to have a drink with me. Cherish has been having your ass tied up for weeks," I stated while daping them up and taking a seat.

"Hey, I'm Annise. Do you want to see the drink menu or do you already know what you want to order?"

"I'll take a Long Island and get them whatever they want."

"So, is everything on you, cuz?" Blaise asked.

"Yea man, I guess."

"Well, in that case, give me three shots of Patron, some boneless buffalo wings, and an order of cheese sticks," he said while looking at me out the corner of his eye.

"Nigga, you're a trip. I guess you can't say free to family or they will run the hell out." We laughed and started chopping it up.

"Have y'all figured out if y'all gone move or not. With all this shit going on and ole boy coming after your girl, it may not be a bad move, if you ask me."

"You're right; if he was able to find her then I'm sure anyone can. I can't have her out here laying bodies down like this. She's too good for that."

"Dang man, my big bruh done fell in love with the black bitch with green eyes." As soon as the word bitch rolled off his tongue, I could see Eazy was about to hit his ass real quick, I think Blaise knew that shit too."

"Don't look at me like that, you know that's sis and I was just playing."

"Yea, I hear you!" Eazy replied, "Anyway, I want to come. Just let me know when you're leaving, I'll have to talk to Cherish and you know she will have to talk to Chloe."

"You let me handle Chloe, that won't be a problem at all. Aye, wait, speaking of problems, how about Dorian hoe ass texted me today."

"She had better get back; Chloe's gone put some lead in her ass!" Blaise yelled out while stuffing a hot wing in his mouth.

"That's what I told her. I let her know I was going to put my pit bull on her ass too. She says she's been living in my condo. Chloe and I are gone slide through there before we go out. I told her if she knows what's good for her, she wouldn't be there."

"Y'all need anything else?" Annise, the waitress, asked.

"Yea I do," Blaise said as he took a napkin and wiped the sauce off his hands. "I'm not giving you any more drinks unless you want some water, you have had one too many already!" she scolded.

"Damn, bruh, shorty sounds like she's your woman or some shit."

"Nah, she ain't! But if she keeps talking to me like that she will be. I love it when a bih… a woman takes control."

"I'm glad you switched that word up," she said.

"So what's up, you gone slide me your number or do I need to sit here until you get off work? Cause I'll do it. I've gotta make sure these niggas don't come at my lady wrong."

"Yea, I want you to sit right there and wait till I get off at seven, then we can go have a drink."

"Aight bet, how about my brother takes me back to my car and I come right back up here."

"Nope, I want you to stay right here till I get off and I'll take you to your car!" she insisted. I'm feeling shorty already, Blaise is a lil' hot head and she looks like she's just the right one to tame his ass.

"Well damn it, I'm sitting right here then," Blaise said, adjusting himself in his seat like he just got scolded by his kindergarten teacher.

"Aight man, you be easy, holla if you need me," Eazy said as we walked out the building.

Shorty's gone make Blaise a new man by tomorrow." Eazy chuckled.

"Right! Hit my line later, I'm about to head to the mall and pick Chloe up something."

"Look at you, getting all soft on me," Eazy said.

"I'm far from soft, I just want to make my girl smile that's it and man, fuck you! Where are you headed?" I asked.

"To Zales!" Eazy yelled and jumped in the car. How is he gone talk about me being soft and he about to go buy Cherish some jewelry. I laughed to myself.

Turning the radio up, speeding down 280 to the mall while this new song by Tank came on and had me thinking about Chloe ass.

Every time I lick it you be losing it, these young boys didn't know what to do with it. You got it all on my face, I love the way that it taste when you put it all on my plate, it won't go to waste. That's what you get every day when you fucking with me. Every day when you wake up, when you get home from your job, trust me bae I don't get tired. I got more than one way to please ya.

"Oh, shit this joint is hot. It makes me want to get to Chloe ass quick and put some dick in her life."

***

Pulling clothes out my closet, I laid out my black slacks, a black button up, a red tie, and my Christian Louboutin velvet loafers out on the bed. Yea, I'm a G, but if your man can't do both you don't need his ass. You can't be hard every day.

Miss Fat Ass: *I hope you're on your way because I miss yo fine ass.*

Me: *Big daddy is on the way, you just make sure you're dressed to kill.* (Literally) She just may be killing someone tonight if Dorian ass still in my shit.

Miss Fat Ass: *I did my best, that's all I can say.*

Me: *Well shit, I'm glad I bought you something to wear. See you in a little bit, ma.*

***

I walked into Eazy's crib just as Cocoa was walking down the stairs. I had bags behind my back to give her as a gift.

"I thought I heard you pull up," she said as she switched down the stairs.

"Are you ready?"

"Yea I'm ready, but you're not! Where are you going with that shit on?" I expressed.

"I thought I told you no thot shit and here you go coming down the stairs all slow like yo ass is in a Tyler Perry movie with a dress with holes going down both sides. If you don't take yo ass back upstairs!" I yelled, making Cherish come out the kitchen. She looked at Chloe and started laughing.

"I told yo ass he wasn't going for that!" she yelled while walking back into the kitchen.

I walked up the stairs behind her only to find her on the bed with an attitude. "What's your problem, ma?"

"I told you I did the best I could do, Cherish and Eazy were gone so I didn't have a way to go buy something else."

"You should have called me bae, don't ever feel like you can't do that. I told you I don't know what you're used to but I'm cut from a different cloth."

"I've never had a man before, well no relationship period. All this is new to me, so in my eyes this was sexy."

"Yea, it's sexy if you about to go make some quick cash." I paused, I shouldn't have said that. I know her history so I'm sure none of those niggas ever did anything special for her, on top of her being only twenty-one years old.

"I'm sorry, I shouldn't have said that. Look here put this on and come back downstairs when you are finished." She smiled at me and I gave her a kiss on the forehead before I walked out the room.

Shortly after I sat down and took a sip of Crown Cherish gave me, Chloe came down the stairs. She had her hair pressed out and it was flowing as she walked down the stairs. I bought her this black Christian Dior Bodycon dress that showed off that banging ass body of hers, and a matching pair of Christian Louboutin, except hers were heels and some Vera Wang perfume. I smelled her before she could even get all the way down the stairs.

"Damn lil' sis, now that's how you make a fucking entrance!" Cherish yelled out while standing up and clapping. "Yaaasss bitch! Yaasss!"

I couldn't do anything but shake my head at her country ass. But my baby was giving me the real definition of bad and bougie. I handed her a single red rose, took her by the arm, and walked out the door. I was feeling like the luckiest man on this planet right now. She was broken when I met her, but I'm here to make her whole again. I'm never the mushy type. Yea, I had women, but I don't give my heart to no bitch, cause those hoes can't be trusted. Lil' mama right here was doing less and some kind of way that made me want to know more and see where this could lead. I should have learned my lesson with Dorian hoe ass but nah, I'll try this shit one more time. Oh, and it doesn't help that she is fine as fuck. She's a cancer so she's hard on the outside but soft on the instead. By her history, I could tell she always wanted to guard her heart so she never got attached to anyone. She treated them like straight hoes, but all that shit had to cease cause now she got a real man in her life and that hoe shit had to go.

Chapter 16

Cocoa

He opened the doors to his truck and helped my short ass climb up in while smacking me on my ass in the process. "Aight bae, you're gone make us go back to your place and say fuck dinner!" I spat as he closed the door behind me.

I love the chemistry we have, he makes a bitch feel like she's Michelle and he's Obama, or Beyoncé and he's Jay Z's fine big lip ass, or I'm Kim K. and he's Kanye. Nah, scratch that last one, I'll just stop at Jay Z. I've never been treated this way before. Usually, it's wham, bam, thank you, ma'am, yo money on the dresser, I'll call you next week. He saw me in a completely different light. He knows all about my past and he still picked me; and for that very reason alone I'm going to suck his dick until the sunrise.

"Cocoa... Cocoa!" he said while snapping his fingers in my face.

"Are you good? You're just staring out the window completely ignoring me as I call your name."

"I'm sorry, babe. I was sitting here thinking how lucky I was to have a guy like you, that's all. Sorry, I didn't mean to ignore you." I apologized, my thoughts of him sometimes have my ass in a trance and I just sit there smiling staring at a wall thinking about him.

"I was saying that I needed to go by my condo to check things out."

"Check things out! Can't that wait until tomorrow?" I asked.

"No, I need to make sure my ex isn't still in my shit. I put her ass out months ago but I forgot to get my key back and she texted today saying she miss a nigga and shit and she's been at the crib waiting for me."

"Oh, now I know the bitch had better not be there when I get there. I want her to tell me how much she misses you, watch I fuck her ass up, and still go eat dinner afterwards. Let's hurry this shit up, I'm not trying to let this ruin our night!" I spat.

After I said hurry up, I could feel the truck taking off down the expressway. I'm glad he knew I was not playing. About five minutes later, we pulled up to his condo downtown. I slowly walked up the stairs behind him and watched him unlock the door. As soon as he opened it, he was pulled in by two guys.

"Ahh man, not tonight!" Stomping on the ground with frustration I yelled out to myself, I really wanted this shit to be peaceful but now it looks like I have to stretch these niggas out. I always keep the gun Rocko gave me at the lake house with me now. Being with these men, I've learned life will be forever unpredictable and you just may have to go to war for them at any moment, like now. I walked up to the door and twisted the knob. It was locked! So I did what any normal girlfriend would do. I called the police after I kicked the damn door in.

They must have had him in the back, cause I only saw her as she jumped up on the couch from the sound of the door coming unhinged. I ran over to her and started delivering blows to her head. The bitch bit my arm hard as fuck. I took my lucky .9mm out and shot the hoe in the head. Hearing scuffling from the back room made me run towards the sound. One of the guys had a gun to Rocko head, and the other one was sitting on the bed rolling a blunt. *I don't know what type of shit this is but I'm about sick and tired of it,* I thought to myself.

"Say good night, wit cho bitch ass," I heard the man say who had the gun pointed at Rocko.

My heart started racing, I pushed the door in and just started shooting. I knew the technique cause my sisters and I loved going to the gun range, but fuck technique at the moment I just started letting rounds off until Rocko and I were the only ones standing.

I ran to him and all he could say was, "Them niggas scuffed up my damn shoes." This man must be crazy as hell; he just had a gun pointing to his head and all he had to say was they scuffed up his shoes.

"You're stupid babe," I said, letting out a little laugh. He grabbed my hand and we left the room.

"Damn what happened to her?" He asked, as he walked around what's her name body on the floor. "Oh she ok, she's not breathing, though. Other than that she's good."

He grabbed me by my waist and led me outside. Sirens were beginning to flash and we sat on the steps until they came up. He explained the story on how his ex had two men tried to kill him and I came in and saved him. I saw my mom's ex pull up on the scene, so

I walked over to him and gave him my version of the story so he would fix this shit too.

"You know you and you sister are gonna get my ass fired. How in the hell am I supposed to keep explaining these damn dead bodies?" He questioned.

"You're the C.O.P. I'm sure you've done a lot worse than cover up some shit for us. Now, I have a date to get to," I stated, patting him on the back.

"Make sure my man's place is cleaned up, we may have to use it in a few hours!" I yelled back to him as I walked towards Rocko.

"Are you ready to enjoy the rest of our night?" He asked.

"Of course, baby, let's go." He picked me up and walked me to his truck.

"You've had a busy night already and I want to preserve some of that energy for later." He picked my lil' thick ass up like I was light as a feather, stiff and a board.

"Thank you," he said while leaning in to kiss me. I turned my head just like he did me when I first tried to kiss him.

"Oh, it's like that now?" He laughed.

"I don't know where your mouth been, you may have the cooties!" I spat in my New-New from *ATL* voice.

"Yo ass is crazy, you better give me those lips."

He grabbed my face and kissed me like no one else was around; he kissed me like they weren't bringing three dead bodies out of his house. It's a shame, I never even asked him her name. For now, we just gonna call her ass Jane Doe. We cruised the city, before stopping at Ruth Chris steakhouse. Being the gentleman he always is, he came around and opened my door for me.

"Thank you, baby," I said as I extended my hand out to him.

He kissed my hand and walked me inside. I was smiling from ear to ear. When I first met him I thought he was so arrogant and his attitude seemed so fucked up. He kind of scared me at first because he's so tall over me, his body is full of muscles and he kind of reminds me of that Instagram guy that workout all the time that's sexy as hell. I think his name is Chadoy Leon; that man is fine as hell and my Rocko looks a lot like him. He has caramel skin, tattoos, a sexy ass full beard, and muscles everywhere. He's 6'0, compared to my 5'4 frame he was a giant. Little did I know that beast in him could be tamed and he was actually the perfect man for me. Although I've killed one, too many damn people since meeting him, I still wouldn't change any of it— except the part where I lost my sister but that was my fuck up.

"You are old enough to drink, right?" he asked, pulling me from my thoughts, "Really? You're just now gone ask me if I'm legal!"

"You better calm yo lil' ass down, you know I was just playing. I know you are barely legal."

"Well, I can't help that yo mama is a freak and had you years before mine had me." His eyes went cold when I mentioned his mom.

"I'm sorry babe, I shouldn't have said anything about your mom."

"It's cool, ma! Go ahead and let the waiter know what you want to eat," he said while looking away from me. I guess his mom is a sensitive subject so I won't ask him about her right now. All I knew is that she was still alive and he never said anything else about her.

"I'll have the Asiago Steak and shrimp, with no shrimp, a house salad with ranch dressing and loaded mashed potatoes with a small cup of ranch dressing on the side." He and the waiter both looked at me like I was crazy.

"Why didn't you just order a steak?" He asked with a confused look on his face.

"Well, babe, looking at this picture on the menu, the cheese looked really good melted on top of the steak and shrimp but I'm allergic to shrimp, so I just want the steak and cheese."

He laughed at me. "You are really something special," I smirked back at him and blew him a kiss. "I'll have the steak and lobster tail, no onions, loaded mashed, a house salad, and make sure you bring A1 sauce out to the table please."

As the waiter walked off to put our order in, he grabbed my hand and just stared at me. "Stop it, you're making me blush." I giggled.

"It's cool I love it when you blush, you look really good tonight too."

"Thanks, my man picked it out," I replied, causing him to smile.

"I like the sound of that. I asked you out to dinner because I wanted to talk to you about something."

"What's wrong? Is everything ok? You didn't bring me here to dump me, right?" I asked question after question before he could even answer the first one I was coming with anything one.

"Calm down, shorty. Now, to answer your questions, nothing is wrong, everything is ok, and no I didn't bring you here to dump you." He laughed and took a sip of his drink.

"So talk to me babe, what's going through your head?"

"I wanted to tell you that when I leave next Friday, I won't be returning. I'm selling my house and my condo. I have a lot of things I need to focus on in New York and running back here to visit you and to check on things every month now is interfering with everything I have going on out there."

My eyes started to fill up with water. He said he wasn't dumping me but this sure as hell felt like a long story to a fast break up to me. "Shorty, what you crying for?"

"Because it sounds like you want this to be some long distance shit!" I spat while folding up my arms.

"Chloe, that's not what I want at all, I actually want you to move with me. That's if you want to, of course."

"Fuck yea, I want to!" I said with pure excitement in my voice. "Wait! But I'll have to leave my sister, and I can't do that."

"Don't worry about your sister, Eazy is coming too and he's asking her tonight as well."

A smile graced my face again and I leaned up to kiss him right as our food arrived at the table.

"This looks delicious," I said as I unfolded my napkin and tucked it into the neck of my dress."

He started laughing out if the blue. "I can tell yo ass ain't never been nowhere before but its ok, I'll teach you."

"What you mean?" I asked with a little attitude. "Chloe, take your napkin and put it on your lap."

"But I don't want to get anything on my dress," I replied.

"Exactly, that's why you place it in your lap. You should never eat so fast that you have food dripping from your chin and if so, you grab your napkin off your lap and wipe your mouth and place it back on your lap."

"Well who died and made you the king of proper fucking etiquette?" I asked as I did what he said.

"Yo mama, cause that's who supposed to teach you things like this." He started to laugh but I didn't find that shit funny at all.

Once we finished our dinner we headed back to his place, for what I'm hoping to be a real nightcap. As soon I got in the truck I could feel the vibration from my phone. I know it can't be anyone but my sister since I got my number changed a few weeks ago.

Sissy Pooh: *Soooo did he ask you yet?*

Me: *About moving?*

Sissy Pooh: *Yea.*

Me: *Yea, I said I'm down, but only if you are coming too.*

Sissy Pooh: *Now bitch, you know I couldn't turn that shit down. Lol.*

Me: *Lol me either, I'm the happiest I've ever been.*

Sissy Pooh: *I know you are and I am extremely happy for you, I know we haven't always seen eye to eye, but you're my baby sister and I will always want nothing less than the best for you and besides Romello's ass look like he can lay the pipe down. Lmaoooo!*

Me: *Bitch bye, I will let you know in the morning! Lol, love ya.*

Sissy Pooh: *Love you too, Chloe Chanel Carter.*

She knows I hate when she call my whole name out like that.

"Who are you over there texting that's got yo ass smiling like that?" Rocko inquired.

"That was my sister, pipe down! Don't nobody want me but you."

"Good and I plan on keeping it that way. Now let me hurry up and get your fine ass home so I can get into those panties," he said, causing both of us to bust out in laughter.

"What panties?"

He looked over at me with the side eye. "Cocoa, don't play. You ain't have no panties on all night?" He asked, reaching over to feel between my legs.

"You ain't gone feel nothing but a freshly waxed pussy," I said while spreading my legs open for him to feel.

Once he touched me my pussy started to get wet. I moved my body so now my knees are in my seat but facing him. I unzipped his pants, pulled his dick out and started sucking it while we were riding down the expressway.

"Shit baby, yo lil' hot mouth ass..." is all he could get out before letting out a moan. "You're gone have to stop, babe. I keep closing my eyes." As soon as he said that I felt a lot of roughness on the road. "Oh shit!" he spat.

"What was that?" I asked. The sound caused me to jump up right as he was coming full force off the side of the road. "You did not really just run off the road." I started laughing,

"That shit ain't funny, we were about to be two dead asses and you would have died with daddy's dick in your mouth!" he spat.

"At least you would have died a happy man."

"Yo ass needs help, for real."

"Whatever, just hurry up and get home!" I spat as I adjusted myself back into my seat. I guess I won't be doing that shit again.

Chapter 17

Eazy

Damn, I haven't heard from Blaise's ass in two days. That's not like him at all. I guess lil' mama from the restaurant has got his ass tied up. I've got so much shit I have to do before we move I don't even have time to fool with him anyway. This move to New York will be big for us. I'm ready to get back to the money. Things have been kind of slow motion here lately. After all that has gone on, I had to put a hold on moving shit. Once we get settled in, I'll get right back to business.

"Hey, baby, Chloe and I are about to have lunch, you want anything back?"

"Nah, I'm good, once I finish this I'm going to ride down on lil' brother to see what's up with him and this move. He met a chick at Applebee's the other day and I haven't heard from his ass since."

"You know Blaise, he probably tied up to somebody bed right now having the time of his life." She walked over and gave me a kiss before walking out the door.

Boom! Boom! Boom!

Who the fuck is knocking on my damn door like that? I grabbed my gun off the table, opened the door, and had it aimed right at Rocko head.

"A nigga's got one more time to put a gun to my head and not pull the trigger."

"You better start announcing yourself then!" I replied to the bullshit he was spitting..

"Put that shit away, and where is Blaise's ass at? We need to get some shit straight before y'all move."

"I haven't seen or heard from him since we left him at Applebee's, I'm about to hit his line and tell him to come over now. You're acting like you got some rules and regulations or some shit. What's up?" I asked after sending Blaise a text to slide through.

"Nah, I just don't want that same shit that happened here to happen when y'all move. You know how Blaise can get and the last thing I need is someone running in the house on me and my ole lady."

"Yea, I feel you. I'm sure Unc can handle Blaise, though."

"Unc? Fuck that nigga got to do with anything! I don't want his ass around, I told you he was on some snake shit before and I ain't spoke to his ass since my dad died."

"Ok cool, I'll make sure to put that nigga on a need to know basis only," I replied.

A few moments later Blaise walked in with Annise the chick from Applebee's grinning from ear to ear. "What's good, fam?" He yelled out.

"I thought I asked you to come alone?" I spoke up, as Blaise came through the kitchen where Rocko and I were.

"Yea you did, but this is family now."

"And how the fuck is she family?" Rocko responded.

"Y'all asses left me up there waiting on her to get off work. After talking to her all night long, I knew I didn't want to go another moment without making her my wife. So, we flew to Vegas and made this thang official. Meet Mrs. Annise Johnson."

I couldn't do anything but shake my head at him. This is exactly what Rocko was worried about. This dumb moves he making. He doesn't know shit about ole girl and he goes and does some dumb shit like this.

"Blaise, I really don't give a damn who she is now, but she needs to sit on the porch and wait until we finish talking."

"Nah, my wife ain't going nowhere."

"How I'm feeling right now Blaise, you can take yo ass back outside with her," I said. Blaise was on some dumb shit right now, this is probably the dumbest shit he has done.

"Eazy, you gotta check him before I say his ass can't come. Real shit E, Blaise can't be trusted with the simplest shit. Family or not I can't have him cause hell up there. Them niggas up there don't play these country games. They respect me and know I'll fuck their world up if they come at me with some bullshit, but as soon as Blaise start acting like he a boss they're gone leave his ass chopped up on your doorstep. He may need to stay where it's slow and steady, that fast life ain't for him!" Rocko stated.

I can't even front and even act like he will do right up there. He shows out here so I can only imagine what he would do there.

"I'll holla at him and let him know he need to get his shit together or it may be best to stay here with his wife," I said, causing me to bust out laughing. "Who the fuck gets married in two days?"

"Yo dumb ass brother obviously. Are you sure Auntie Daneese wasn't getting a check for him?"

"Man, hell no!"

"You know she had a gambling problem so she probably was, y'all just didn't see it," Rocko said, causing me to look at his ass sideways.

"Leave my momma and her habits alone, Bruh cause Auntie Delisa was right alone with her at those tables. Did she ever get y'all house back she lost? Right! You can't answer that shit, huh? Anyway, I'm about to finish packing up the last of my things so I can ship it up there and I'll holla at you later on. Tell Blaise's ass he can come in if he still outside."

"Say B, yo brother said get cho bitch made ass in the house before he set yo bitch's weave on fire!" he yelled out.

Now, this man knows damn well I didn't say all that. If you asked me both of them could be getting a good ass check.

"What's up man?" Blaise said.

"Shit, what the fuck is wrong with you? You've been moving real funny since ole boy knocked yo ass out." I love my lil' brother but I can't let him come between me and my money.

"Nothing I'm good, or at least I'll be fine when we get to New York."

"Oh nigga, ain't no New York for you. Since you wanna run off and get married, you stay yo ass here and take care of your wife. When I move ain't no more traffic flow this way. That shit stops so you better ask ole girl if they have a job for a cook!" I yelled.

"Oh, it's gone be like that? I guess Rocko put you up to this shit. It's cool, I'll be ok! Tell sis I'll holla at her some other time. I'm out and lose my fucking number. Let's go, babe," he said to his wife, grabbing her hand and slamming the door behind him.

Me: *Bring your ass home; daddy needs some of that good shit.*

Baby Girl: *Shut up, boy I'm about to pull in. Go wash your dick; I know it's all sweaty and shit. Lol*

Me: *My dick is always clean.*

She walked into the house throwing her bags down and started running up the stairs. "Baaaaby, where are you?"

"I'm downstairs."

"What? Why did you watch me run all the way up those damn stairs?"

"Yo thick ass can stand to run around a block or two!" I cried out, making her laugh and show her deep dimples. "Bring that ass here."

She had on this short romper that made her ass look even fatter. She unzipped the front of it, and I sat there watching it fall to the floor. Underneath she wore this red lace thong set. Walking over to me I couldn't help but admire how beautiful she was. Her hair was in one of those knots on the top of her head, what y'all women like to call that shit, a bun. Whatever it is I'm about to take that shit down, I like her hair wild when I'm fucking her. She dropped her panties down to the floor, then straddled me on the couch, I unhooked her bra and threw it on the floor. Cuffing her breasts in my hand, I started gently sucking causing her to moan softly. Squeezing on her ass, I lifted her up and pulled my dick out. She dropped down to her knees and eased my dick into her mouth. Shorty had the wettest mouth I've ever felt. I pulled her hair back off her face so I could watch her take my dick like a pro. She started stroking it, and then she spits on the head and climbed on top of me. Feeling my dick go inside her tight ass pussy, I grabbed her by the waist and pulled her down on my dick, as I stroked deeper inside of her.

"Fuck, baby, shit... right there!" she moaned out while grinding faster on my dick making me damn near lose control.

"Aight, ma you're gone make a nigga bust all in that pussy."

"Hmmm, cum with me."

As soon as she said that I felt her pussy start to tighten up around my dick, as nut instantly started shooting inside her, while she creamed all on my dick. "Yea, that ass is mine for real now," I said while pulling her face to me and giving her a kiss on the forehead.

"Whatever, I was yours already."

"I know but this time my babies are gone be growing inside of you."

"Babies?"

"Yea, I'm sure that shit I just shot off in you definitely was strong as hell and liable to produce 2-3 kids."

"That's a fucking lie, who's having all those kids at once?

Climbing off me, I watched her ass jiggle as she ran upstairs to the shower.

"You better bring your ass in here to join me while you sitting there mesmerized by this ass!" she spat, causing me to run up the stairs behind her.

Chapter 18

Ce-Ce

2 months later

Everything has been going great since we moved. My sister and I both left our old ways behind us and started a new life. Of course, we didn't want to live in our men shadows, so we both started school again. Chloe should be done by the beginning of next year with her cosmetology license and I have one semester left, then I will be done with my nursing program. When I started taking on the role of a full-time mother to my sisters, or so it seemed like I was; I had to put nursing on hold and took care of my family. With only one semester left I did what I had to do. It was a good thing they allowed all of my credits to transfer, except a few.

Eazy has been a great support system on my journey to become a registered nurse. He said, "Whatever you have to do to keep you from that fraud shit you were doing, I have your back 100%."

Rocko has been teaching him how shit works around here, so some days he does not come home until late at night. I'm sure all of that will change in a few months cause I will definitely need him around the house more often.

Knock! Knock!

That must be Cocoa she was supposed to come by after class.

"Hey, boo."

"Hey, big sis! How are my nieces or nephews or niece and nephew doing?" she asked while rubbing my stomach.

Oh, yea Eazy's ass knocked my ass up just like he said and it's definitely two lil' people growing inside of me. You know that song that says that a lil' pussy's got some power; well, his nut had some power.

"Girl, move. Did you bring me some food since you act like you care so damn much?"

"You know I did," she said while tossing me a steak and cheese from Subway.

"I hope you didn't forget the extra chipotle sauce, that shit is so good," I said while unwrapping my sandwich like it was Christmas wrapping paper.

"Uh uh, girl stop, you are not that hungry." She laughed as I took a big bite and had sauce running down the side of my mouth. "That don't make no damn sense, CeCe!" she spat, shaking her head at me. "Where's Eazy?"

"You already know, he in those streets with yo man. He should be home early today cause I told him I needed my feet rubbed. He tried to send me to the spa, but I'd rather have his ass here catering to me since he is the reason my ass is tired all the damn time."

"Shit, I would have chosen the spa, instead of sitting in this big ass house alone!" Cocoa spat.

My house really is big; he let me pick it out as soon as we arrived. It's five bedrooms, four and a half bath, an indoor pool and hot tub. I love to swim and you guys know it can get cold as hell up here and from what I've heard, the snow ain't no joke. So on those days, I can't go out, I can still take my ass right downstairs to my heated pool. Yesterday he surprised me with a new car. He claims his reason is because our family is expanding, but I think he just wanted me out of his car. I can't be mad cause that brand new GLS63 all black Benz SUV is nasty as hell. My babies and I are going to look so good hopping out that bad boy.

"I'm about to go into one of these damn bedrooms and take a nap," Cocoa said, interrupting my thoughts.

"Just don't take yo ass to any of the bedrooms to the left of the hallway; those are my babies' room!" I yelled out to her as she reached the top of the stairs.

"I'm sure they wouldn't mind Auntie lying in there."

"Nah they wouldn't, but I would! Go into the guest room or go home, hell!" I spat, causing her to laugh cause she knew I really didn't want her to go home.

This has become our daily routine and I enjoyed being around her and hated when she left. I still wished Karma was here with us. I'm sure she is looking down smiling at how close we have become and it sad that it had to take her death to make it happen.

My sister hated to be dirty so burying her wasn't even an option for me. I had her cremated and put her inside an urn that looked like a stack of bibles and placed her on my mantle. I tried finding our mom before we moved away and I came up with nothing. She wasn't in any of the rehabs and I didn't see her on the street, so my only thoughts were that she overdosed and could be lying up inside someone's abandoned building. All I could do was pray and hope her soul makes it halfway to heaven before the devil pulled her back to reality.

Y'all didn't think I would pray her soul made it to heaven after the shit she put her flesh and blood through, did y'all? I can't lie like I don't miss the old her, but I can't even fantasize about that because when reality kicked in, I would remember she was the biggest crackhead known to man. She was worse than Chris Rock when he played that crackhead in *New Jack City*. There was no one to blame but herself, so I no longer feel bad for her. My sister and I were now living the good life and I can finally say "job well done" to myself for raising me and my sisters to be outstanding women. Yea, I know Chloe was slanging pussy like a nigga was slanging his mixtape on the corner, but she grew past that and learned her lesson after Karma died.

"Chloe, wake yo ass up. I know you didn't think I was going to let you sleep for hours. Come down here and massage my feet!" I yelled upstairs into my twins' room that she took her ass in to sleep anyway.

"Yo ass could have let me sleep a little longer and hell no, I'm not about to massage your feet! We about to get in that brand new truck of yours and go to the nail shop. Let those Ching Chong people do that shit cause I ain't! she spat while grabbing my truck keys and my purse.

"Can you at least tie my shoe?" I asked she came over and dropped some flip flops in front of me. I don't know if it was these babies inside of me or what, but I almost wanted to cry because I really wanted to wear my Huaraches and she was being really mean.

"Ce, I know yo ass is not over there crying about no damn shoes. I can't wait till you drop these babies cause I can't do these tears!" she spat while grabbing my purple Huaraches from by door and putting them on my feet.

"I still need you to put my flip flops in that big ass purse of yours so I won't mess my toes up putting these shoes back on." I had to laugh on the inside because she just looked at me like she wanted to kill me.

"Bitch, bye!" she spat and walked out the door.

I love being extra with her. If my sister Karma was here she would have loved to help me. Grabbing her urn off the mantle, I gave her a kiss before walking out of the door. We jumped in my truck and headed towards the nail shop.

Chapter 19

Blaise

I've been sitting around this house pissed for months. My brother and I have always been tight like Mike and Ike. He never left me behind before so I knew this had to be Rocko's doing. My girl and I have been thinking of ways to get back at his ass, though. Call me grimy all you want to, but I don't let nobody fuck me over. You stopped my money from coming in, so watch me stop yours. Nigga won't be able to eat without asking me for money.

"Annise, come over here and take daddy's mind off this bullshit!" I yelled up the stairs at her.

I had to move in with her since Eazy left. She had a five bedroom three bath home with gated entry. Now looking at lil' mama you wouldn't think she was caked up like this. She only worked at Applebee's to pass the time away. Her daddy had long money and after talking to her for a minute I found out her daddy is the plug. I still haven't worked my way up to asking her to link us up. I'll get to that sooner or later, but right now I needed her on my dick like yesterday.

"What's up, daddy?" she said as she walked down the stairs with absolutely nothing on.

My dick instantly started to get rock hard. Annise was the true definition of a true big beautiful woman. She looked like that fine ass bitch, Jasmine Sullivan. She was brown skin, 5'7, and 215 pounds in all the right places.

"Bring that ass here, girl!" I spat, slapping her on the ass and pulling her down on the couch so that she's facing me.

I started sucking her big juicy ass breasts, I love the sound of her moans in my ear. Lifting her up I laid her back on the couch and wrapped her legs around my neck and dove head first into that pussy. Licking her clit and slowing nibbling down and inserted my tongue, I started tongue fucking her ass. I started grabbing her thighs and pulling her closer to my face. I'm not sure what lil' mama's been eating but all I tasted was peach cobbler as she busted on my face.

"Damn shorty, I can eat that ass all day."

"I know you can but right now I want that dick," she whispered softly in my ear. She pushed me back on the floor and climbed on top of me and slowly slid down on my dick. Her pussy was so tight and warm, my eyes instantly started to roll to the back of my head.

"Fuck Annise, slow down you bout to make me cum all in yo ass," I moaned as she gripped my dick with her pussy and started grinding.

"You like that, daddy? Shit... ooooh shiiiit, this feels so fucking good," she moaned while she bit her bottom lip. I grabbed her by the waist and started bouncing her on my dick making her cum all over me.

"Take this dick, take this dick," I repeated, beating her pussy up more as I came inside of her.

"Mommy, mommy can I have some cereal?" her five-year-old son asked as he ran into the living room, causing us to cover up real quick. Oh yea, I forgot to mention shorty had a lil' shorty of her own. A five-year-old some name Gemini.

"Yea baby, mommy will be there in a minute. Now go back into your room like a big boy and I'll call you when it's ready," she replied, making him run back upstairs into his room.

"You know we can't be fucking anywhere in the house," she said as she laughed and threw a couch pillow at my head.

"His lil' bad ass should've stayed in the room like you asked him," I replied and threw the pillow back at her ass.

She had my head gone for real. I couldn't do anything but watch her juicy ass jiggle as she walked back into the bedroom. I needed to get back to thinking of a plan anyway to fuck Rocko how he fucked me.

***

The next day

Riding around the city, I decided to call up Uncle Jimmie to see how he feels about this little situation. He let me in on a lot of shit that I didn't even know about, so now this is becoming bigger than what I was thinking about doing. It looks like my shorties and I will be moving to New York after all.

I don't know the extent of the plans my uncle was coming up with and honestly, I don't give a damn. I tried reaching out to my brother just to check on him and sis, but this nigga never has time for me anymore so I'm about to stop fucking with his ass too.

Ring! Ring!

"Damn, speaking of the damn devil," I said aloud as I answered the phone.

"What's up sis, it's been a minute since you hit my line. What's good?" I asked Cherish.

"Hey baby boy, it has been a minute. I miss yo ass for real, I can't wait to see you again. Oh and I'm not sure if you have talked to Eazy yet, but you've got a set of twin nieces or nephews on the way," she stated in an exciting tone.

"Noooo damn, that's what's up sis, I'm happy for you two. I haven't heard from Eazy since he left. I tried reaching out to him, but he is always hella busy."

"Yea, he is always gone from the house with Rocko. You're straight, though, right? Do you need anything?"

"Nah I'm good, even though he left me fucked up here. I'm still gone make a way and it also helps that my girl got bread falling out her ass," I said, making us both laugh.

"You better not be using her ass Blaise or I'ma beat that ass myself."

"Just know if we ever break up I'm calling yo ass first so we can do her how you did Eazy," I said followed with a laugh.

She probably thought that was a joke, but I promise you, I'ma have sis swipe all that shit. My brother already left me with shit and if she leaves, I'll be damned if I go back to being broke Blaise. I love her but what's love got to do with it?

"I am not about that life anymore Byron Blaise Johnson," she blurted, calling me by my whole name.

"What I tell you about that shit? Sis, it's just Blaise. I don't know if you watched the movie *The Strange Thing About the Johnsons*, but I do not, I repeat do not, want to be associated with any Johnson anymore. So from here on out forget anything else you knew about me," I implied.

"Boy, I saw that sick ass movie and surely you aren't related to them. With yo crazy ass, I can't believe you even compared your family to that shit."

"I don't know about y'all but I'm usually into freaky shit, but when the son started raping his dad I had to turn that shit off quick."

"Boy, you got me dying laughing over here. You still ain't got no damn sense. Your brother is walking in now, do you want to talk to him?" I should but he never returned my phone call from a week ago so I'm good on his ass.

"Nah sis, I'ma let you get to your man, though. You be easy," I said as I hung up the phone.

Just thinking about the good life they are living up there, started to piss me off all over again. It had the wheels turning in my head dying to find out what Unc's got in store for them. I know all about Uncle Jimmie trying to take the business from Rocko, although that shit is foul, I really don't give two fucks. They always want to try me and play me like I'm some soft ass boy who can't handle his own. We will see who will be begging for help when I finish with his ass.

Chapter 20

Rocko

"Cocoa, baby, wake up!" I yelled as I shook her to wake her up.

"What's wrong, baby? I'm sleepy as hell you know how I hate for anyone to wake me up."

"Chloe baby, you're bleeding get up now!" I screamed. She jumped up and saw she was lying in a pool of blood. She instantly panicked and started crying.

"Rock, what the hell is this,? Oh my gosh!" she screamed out while running to the bathroom.

"Fuuuuuuuuck!" she yelled as she sat on the toilet in pain.

"Baby, come on so I can get you to the hospital."

Seeing her in so much pain had me damn near in tears, especially since I don't know what the fuck is going on. I started running her a shower to clean herself up before we left and all she did was lay down in the tub and cry out for me to help her. I didn't know what else to do so I called 911. I unlocked the door and ran back to the bathroom and got in the tub with her. All I could do was hold her to get her to calm down till the ambulance came. About ten minutes went by and they finally came running through the door.

"We are in the bathroom!" I yelled out to them. Before they got there I went and grabbed her some clothes to put on. Even though she was in pain, I didn't want them seeing my girl's goodies.

"What happened?" one of the EMT women asked.

"I don't know, when I came home she was lying in a pool of blood and I called you guys because she wouldn't let me take her to the ER," I stated as I watched them load her up on the stretcher and attempt to start an IV. By this time, she's crying hysterically and they had to tie her down to the bed. Seeing her like that made me lose my mind.

"Cherish, meet me at the hospital ASAP, something is wrong with Chloe!" I yelled through the receiver.

I jumped into my car and followed closely behind the ambulance. I could see them working on her through the windows of the back door. As soon as we stopped, I got out the car and ran through the doors. They rolled her to the back and made me wait up front.

"I have to make sure she's good!" I screamed at one of the nurses who started pushing me back.

"Romello, what happened?" Cherish asked as she ran up to me.

"Man, Cherish, I don't know. All I know is she was really bloody and in pain. They won't let me back there with her because I'm not her husband!" I stated and started punching the walls.

"Calm down, they will let me back there." She turned and walked towards the nurses' station. Moments later, the doors opened up and she ran to the back leaving me and Eazy up front waiting.

"I can't lose her Eazy, that's my world. If something happened to her, I wouldn't know what to do."

Everything started running through my head trying to think of what could be wrong. Tears started falling from my eyes as I started thinking about how life would be without her. They might as well go ahead and take me out too because she not leaving me.

Hours had passed and Cherish finally emerged from the back. I ran up to her only to see her eyes looking like she had been crying.

"Is she ok?" I asked in a voice I didn't even recognize.

"Yes, she's doing fine, but the baby didn't make it."

"Baby? What damn baby?"

"The doctors said she was six weeks pregnant. They had to do a DNC on her to clean her out. They checked her cervix and saw that it was short and she wouldn't have carried the baby full term."

My heart dropped into the pit of my stomach and at that moment all I wanted to do was be with my baby, to comfort her and let her know that daddy is right here and will always be right here for her. I walked into the room and saw her laying there peacefully sleeping. I kissed her forehead and sat in the chair next to her and stared at her until the sun came up.

***

Hearing the sound of the doors open woke me up out of my slumber. I looked over at Chloe and she was still sleeping. They checked her vital signs, left her breakfast and a pain pill.

"Hey, baby," I said as soon as I saw her trying to open her eyes.

"Are you feeling ok? Do you need anything? Are you in pain?" I asked question after question trying to make sure my baby was good. She attempted to sit up and I could see the pain in her eyes so I hurried over to help her.

"Thank you, baby," she whispered in a soft tone. "I'm ok, just tired, I feel real weak. They told me what was wrong. My mind was blown away. I didn't even know I was pregnant. He said my cervix was short and probably by me standing up in class all day and trying to exercise this ass off caused me to miscarry." I saw the tears filling up in her eyes.

"Don't start blaming yourself for this. You couldn't have known this was going to happen," I said as I kissed her forehead. It hurts cause that was our first child and she or he was just ripped away from us in the blink of an eye.

"Good morning Ms. Carter, you gave us quite a scare when you came in last night," Dr. Davidson said as he entered the room. You lost a lot of blood, so we had to give you two blood transfusions. I'm going to send you home with pain pills and I'm putting you on bedrest for two weeks. After that, you can go back to light workouts until you build yourself up to do more. My number is at the bottom of the paper, so if you have any problems please do not hesitate to call the office. Do you guys have any questions?"

"Yea, I do! Do you know if this will happen every time she gets pregnant?" I asked.

"I can't really say if it will or not because I'm not God. As a doctor I can say it may not be safe for her to get pregnant with her cervix being short, but if she does there are certain precautions we can take to make sure she have a healthy delivery. She may be on bedrest the entire time but at least the baby will be safe. Now, if there's nothing else, I'll leave your discharge papers here and you can leave whenever you are ready," he said as he left out the room.

Hearing him say it was a possibility she could have another kid gave me some relief. I wasn't trying to have a kid, but after hearing this it made me wonder how it would be to have little bad ass kids running around the house. I looked over at Chloe and she was already halfway dressed.

"Damn baby, you're not gone wait till the nurse takes the IV out your arm? Sit cho ass down somewhere. What the hell are you in a rush to leave for?" She was really about to piss me off, knowing damn well she just lost a baby and she's up here acting like ain't shit happen.

"I'm ready to get out this damn hospital and get in my bed, this shit is hard as hell. It's got my damn ass hurting."

She let out a little laugh but I could tell she was really hurting on the inside. But if she wanted to laugh to keep from crying, then I'll be Kevin Hart, Mike Epps and Katt Williams' crazy ass for her until she gets tired of me. Shortly after the nurse finally came in and removed her IV and before the nurse could grab the wheelchair, she was halfway out the door. I couldn't do anything but shake my head at this damn woman.

I helped her in the car, went to Walgreens to pick up her medicine and did the dash back to our place. I carried her into the house only to see Cherish and Eazy sitting on our couch eating breakfast.

"Hey, love!" Cherish yelled out as she walked over to Chloe and gave her a hug.

"I made you guys breakfast, I wasn't sure if you wanted your pancakes light, dark or fluffy," she said, causing Chloe to laugh. I guess that was an inside joke between them.

"You're so silly girl, we've really watched *A Thin Line Between Love and Hate* too many damn times."

Chloe helped her to the couch as I went over to the kitchen and fixed her a plate of fruits and some orange juice. I have some things to do so I hope she doesn't trip when Eazy and I slide out the door.

"Here you go, baby," I said as I put the food on the table and sat down next to her.

"You can go Romello, I'm sure you and Eazy have better things to do. "

"Baby, nothing is more important than you right now. If you need me here, I'll stay and we can handle that lil' issue later," I stated.

"Bye, boy! I have my sister here to help me with whatever I need." I caught that side eye from Cherish. That 'don't be all day look' causing me to laugh a little

"I've got you, sis, don't worry I won't be all day," I said without her even saying a word.

Eazy and I walked out the door and dipped over to my connect's crib to finish this deal up with him. I turned my music up and did the dash the whole way there. We pulled up to my connect's Diablo crib and quickly made our way through the front gates. After they removed our guns we were able to take a seat at the round table with him.

"I worked with your father for a long time," he spoke with his Spanish accent.

"He was a very loyal man. I could remember you coming with him a few times as a kid. "Go Getem" is what they called you. So tell me what can I do for you?"

"I wanted to link up, I figured you could be beneficial to me, as I to you. I'm sure you know why they called me that as a youngster. I'm ten times worse than that now. Let me be that guy for you. I mean I'm sure you have men for your dirty work, but you don't have one like me."

"So, the deal is I give you coke and in exchange, you become my personal hitman?" he questioned. I could see the look on Eazy face. Like I said before, I never told him about this part but since he's here he might as well see how I really make my money.

"Exactly."

"Ok, I have a test run for you. If you can do this without getting caught and shit coming back to me, then I'll work with you."

He slid me an envelope and as I opened it a smile graced my face as I read the name, address and what body part he wanted in return.

"Say no more; see you in a week tops." I dabbed him up and left.

The ride back home was silent as "Draco" by Future beamed through the speakers. I know Eazy wanted to ask me more about what just happened, but he just vibed out to the music.

"I'll get at you tomorrow, bruh."

"Aight cool." He dabbed me up before walking into the house. I did the dash all the way to the crib. Just thinking about the envelope had me on edge and ready to show Diablo I'm all about business and most importantly, my paper.

Chapter 21

Cocoa

I love the hell out of this man of mine; just looking at him makes me all moist and shit. I never thought I could settle down coming from where I have been with guys. It's usually not too many men who would take a chance on a woman like me. They say you can't make a hoe a housewife, but I beg to differ because Rocko has definitely proven that statement to be as false as some of these hoes hair.

We are in the car heading over to his uncle's house. I can tell by the look on his face he really didn't want to go. His grandmother called and fussed at him about coming to see her and made him stop by his uncle's house too. So here we are and this nigga is really taking his precious time getting there. I'm talking about literally driving like a turtle.

"You might as well speed up and get this shit over with," I said because as slow as he was driving, he had my ass falling asleep.

"That's because I really don't want to take my ass over here."

He finally sped up and did the dash the rest of the way there. We pulled up to his uncle's house and I must admit I was impressed. I mean it wasn't as big as ours but it was aight for what it was. We were greeted at the door by who I am assuming is the butler. He walked us through the lower part of the house and lead us straight to the backyard where they had a barbecue going. As for now, no one was out here but us. To pass the time away, I did the only logical thing to do to ease his mind a little.

"You like that, daddy?" I asked Rocko while I inhaled his dick even deeper down my throat.

"Shit, lil' mama you know I love dat shit." His eyes started to roll to the back of his head, that's when I knew he was loving this shit for real.

"This shit is cumming babe, fuuck!" he moaned out.

I started stroking his dick and sucking the head like I was bobbing for apples causing him to release in my mouth. Of course, I swallowed it, you know what they say "a lady never spits, she swallows" and I did just that. Grabbing a napkin off the table, I wiped the corners of my mouth. I couldn't meet his uncle for the first time with cum around my mouth. Like I said, I love to please my baby regardless of where we are. If he didn't care we were in his uncle's backyard, why should I? The doors to the patio opened pulling me from my thoughts.

Out walks his uncle's wife, she was absolutely gorgeous, I couldn't help but stare into her eyes. They were greenish brown, that went so well with her almond skin tone. But the more I looked at her, the more my body started to fill up with rage.

"Hello, I'm Jimmie's wife, Cynthia but you can call me Cindy," she stated as she reached her hand out to Rocko.

"Nice to meet you as well," I said, reaching my hand out and knocking Rocko's back down. "I'm Cocoa, and this is MY MAN, ROMELLO."

He laughed like he just knew I was going to pop her old ass if she even held his hand too long. I don't trust females around my man and especially not this one. She had this look on her face like she was disgusted with how rude I had been but I brushed that shit off. In the streets, that shit would've gotten her ass killed, but since we are in his uncle's house I'll let her make it.

"Your uncle should be out shortly, he had to finish up some things first," she stated as she took a sip of her water and sat down across from us.

She had on this short white romper that made her curves show, her legs were toned like she goes hard in the gym, her hair was long and curly, and she had this long flowery sheer cover up on, that flowed in the wind as she walked. She kind of look like Jada Pickett Smith.

"So, how long have you been living here?" I asked.

"Babe, don't ask personal questions like that," Rocko stated before she could even answer. I looked at him and instantly rolled my eyes because I really wanted an answer.

"You guys look really good together." I guess she is going to completely ignore my question.

"Thanks, I only fuck with the best of them," Rocko said as he looked over, grabbed my hand and gave me a gentle squeeze. "Y'all have a nice little set up over here, it's a shame I've never been to Unc's place as close as we used to be."

"Yea, it is a shame but even teeth and tongue fall out, so whatever differences you guys had, I'm sure we can get past all that and make this one big happy family. Your uncle and I have been together for two years now and he has always mentioned his nephews Rocko, Eazy and Blaise."

"Yea that's good to hear, but my number never changed. I haven't heard from him since my dad died five years ago. So I didn't just lose my dad, I lost my uncle too; they meant everything to me and he knew that. He was all I had left besides my cousins and he still stopped fucking with me so I'm not sure what he told you, Miss Lady, but seems like it wasn't nothing but bullshit to make himself look good!" Rocko spat back at her.

I was glad he was putting her in her place. How dare she try to have an input on someone else's family that ain't have shit to do with her.

"Well, we can just move past that and I will let you two handle y'all business as men and work this shit out." As soon as she said that, the patio doors opened again, I assumed it was his uncle. He walked up to us and reached out for a hug from Rocko and he just sat there. My nigga can't even fake kick it with his family, I laughed on the inside at that shit. Uncle Jimmie is in his mid-50s and looked all of 40, nice clean cut, smooth light skin and he smelled so damn good.

"Damn nephew, your favorite uncle can't get a hug, handshake, or shit, huh?" he asked with his hands still held out.

"Favorite uncle? Who is that? My favorite uncle wouldn't have gone ghost on my ass when pops died. I only came by cause I told granny I would."

"At the end of the day, we're still family and whatever happened back then I'm hoping we can move past that."

"Maybe, we will see," Rocko said as he adjusted himself in his seat

"Who is this beautiful lady sitting next to you? I'm Romello a.k.a. Go Getem's uncle," he said, extending his hand out to me. Rocko looked at me with the coldest eyes, I already knew that meant to keep my arms folded.

"That's my girl Chloe, and only family calls me "Go Getem"!" he said with clenched teeth before I could say anything. I could see her starting to look funny in the face when he said my name, but she never said anything so he just continued on talking.

"Ok, ok. I can respect that," Uncle Jimmie said with his hands up surrender style

"Ok, before this get out of hand, let's change the subject. So, do you guys have any kids together?" she asked as she sat back and crossed her legs.

"No, Cocoa actually can't have kids," Rocko said as he looked over at me.

That was always a sensitive subject but because of how I was as a child, I got pregnant a few times and always made my way to the clinic for an abortion. I couldn't let a baby come between me and my paper I was chasing. I didn't know the consequences I would face later about it. The doctor explained to me what was wrong with my ovaries and how I couldn't carry kids and if I did get pregnant, I would have to be on bedrest the entire pregnancy. Rocko acted like he was ok with not having kids as long as he had me that was enough, but I know it still bothered him a little cause hell, it even bothered me. I would love to have a little Cassie or Rocko Jr. running around here.

"Oh, that's not good, but who knows what God has in store for you? Doctors may say NO but God's YES can overpower that any day. Your uncle and I would love to have some little nieces or nephews to spoil, you two would have beautiful kids," she said, smiling looking over at us. After she said that, I could no longer keep my composure.

"What the fuck do you know about kids? You haven't seen yours in four years, so tell me how in the hell have you been... mother?" I exclaimed.

When I saw her walk out those doors my heart dropped into my stomach. I hadn't seen my mom in four years and the last time I saw her, she was a fucking crackhead and living on the streets, or so we thought. She looked exactly like Cherish that's how I knew who she was the closer she walked up to us. The fucked up part was she didn't even notice her own child looking back at her. Then to discuss kids when she is the reason I can't have any. Yes, I blame this on her because if she never started me fucking for her to get a quick fix then my body would still be pure, but instead, I'm half of a woman because of that shit.

"Cocoa, what the hell are you talking about?" Rocko blurted out.

"You know the bum bitch I told you about that abandoned her daughters for drugs? Yea. this is that bitch! She's sitting up here talking about nieces and nephews, well bitch guess what they would be your fucking grandkids!" I yelled as the tears started to fill up in my eyes.

"Chloe?" she said with the look of surprise on her face. "Is that you, baby girl?"

"Fuck that, don't baby girl me."

"Aye, watch your fucking mouth, I'm still your mother."

"You ain't shit to me. We thought you were dead and right now I really wish you were."

Who the fuck does she think she is, you can't chastise a child you didn't raise, she gave up on us a long time ago. It's too late to try to be a parent now. I was so fucking pissed off and before I knew it, I pulled my gun out and put it to her head.

"Why? All I want to know is why? You've never tried to contact us, you've been out here living the fucking good life with butlers and shit, while your kids are out here getting it by any means. You need to explain this shit and quickly!" I said with the gun still to her head.

"Her kids? Fuck you mean! You never told me you had kids."

"Jimmie, let me explain!" Cindy yelled out.

"Oh ok, so you want to explain shit to him but not me, your own fucking child? You know what, FUCK YOU!" I spat as I lifted the gun back up towards her head.

Pow!

TO BE CONTINUED...

Made in the USA
Lexington, KY
09 November 2017